Sea Hawk,
Sea Moon

Beverley Birch

**Hodder
Children's
Books**

a division of Hodder Headline

5375,101,

Contents

For Margaret and Rolfe
who will know this place,
with thanks

PART ONE

SEA HAWK

One

Ben saw them for the first time together – the boat and the girl – and they were forever after joined in his mind. He came through the trees; below was the bay scooped from the side of a green hill and the boat leaning on the sand, and the girl standing by the boat. Her hands rested on its broad belly.

Suddenly she grasped the sloping edge of the wood and with a single, easy movement vaulted up and over and in, straightening as she landed to gaze out across the loch.

There was nothing to see in the sea mists that gusted in on the strengthening wind.

There *was* the shrill cry of a bird, and Ben could see it wheeling above her – and beyond, where boulders massed in a dark ridge thrusting out into the water, he could see the serried ranks of others, betrayed by the spread and shake of a wing.

But the girl was not facing the birds, and Ben wondered what she was looking at, or searching for, or listening to.

He shifted the weight of his backpack, easing the straps where they rubbed his shoulders. He thought about putting it

3

down and sitting for a moment to catch his breath.

Because even then – at the beginning, before any of it had begun – there was something in the boat and the girl that had caught him.

Did he know it? Certainly later, when it was all over and he stood looking down at the girl's still face, willing her to open her eyes, willing her to return to them, it was always to that first morning that his mind returned. To that misty bay, and the dark bulk of the boat, and the girl vaulting into it.

He remembered how he wanted to stay. He remembered the slow shifting sweep of waters bounded by the tongue of boulders on one side and the rocky headland on the other. He remembered moving to a fallen tree and sitting down.

From that angle he saw the darkness along the side of the boat, that it was not shadow but a hole, low and long. With surprise he realised that this was Michael's boat, the one that Michael had written about in his letter.

But Michael had said nothing about the girl.

Now she turned back, paused, then swung down as lightly as she had leapt up. She stooped to something on the beach, slung it over her shoulder and ran across the sands into the shallows, flicking up water with her feet, crossing the bay in a long, splashy line, the frothy path of her passing lit by a stab of pale sunlight through the mist. The ray broadened and warmed, advancing across the sands till it touched the boat at one end and the girl at the other.

He watched her bright shape climb between the rocks on

the far headland, dwindling rapidly against the immensity of the green hill and the mountains beyond.

She was gone. And now that she was, Ben was tempted to go down into the bay. But it was an hour since he had left the ferry – a growl of hunger in his stomach reminded him of the sandwiches he'd eaten at dawn in the coach station at Glasgow, and before that the long sleepless haul on the night train from London. He took a bottle of water from the pack and drank deeply. The mist was lifting; the bay glowed with the brightening sun and the wind buffeting him was warm. The boat rested, glistening with the moisture in the air. It would still be there later.

He dragged the pack on to the tree trunk and slid his arms through the straps, cursing the weight. Three heavy books on wooden ship restoration that Michael had asked for, not one shorter than three hundred pages.

Though Ben didn't really mind. Not now he'd seen the boat.

He moved back to the footpath and resumed his trek. How much further *was* it to Michael's place? The ferryman had said it was an hour's walk, but there was no sign of it yet – or of any other house.

Here the path forked: the left finger pointed down to the loch, the right stayed high and curved towards the road skirting the bay below the hill. Now all he wanted was to find Michael's place, put the pack down at last, and stop.

He settled into a steady pace towards the road. He

wondered if the girl was someone Michael knew or just a passing stranger. He wondered if he'd see her again. The boat lingered, just on the edge of his vision, just there, in a waiting corner of his mind.

But he was unprepared, when he emerged from a shallow copse of trees on the headland, for the girl still being there. She sat cross-legged on a ledge of rock, binoculars to her eyes, intent on the water below. His boots crunched on the path and she swung round, startled.

Ben hesitated. He saw the hint of alarm in her face. He saw she didn't expect anyone else on that path.

He should say something.

His mind went blank.

She'd sprung to her feet with a decisive air that said, I can move faster than you, and I will if I have to. The action untied his tongue and he said quickly, 'Sorry . . . I'm looking for a cottage . . . My uncle's, Michael—'

'Oh—!' The smile flooded her face. 'You're Ben!' Something caught her attention and she swung to face the loch again, lifting the binoculars to her eyes. 'They're back,' she said cryptically. 'See – just below. Quick, or they'll go.' She freed the binocular strap from her wild hair and held the glasses out to him.

Nonplussed, Ben took them. Without ceremony she shoved him forward and pointed.

A ring of black shapes. Moving, in steady formation, outwards from the shore towards a line of rocks in the water.

'They've not been this way for years. They used to come by here,' the girl said. There was a light Scottish burr to her tones. 'Then they just stopped. Now they're back . . .'

Infected by her interest, Ben studied them through the glasses. Glossy dark curves. The point of a snout. One turned, looked back. As if at them, as if listening to their voices. Sunlight caught the sheen of water on the head and spun a sparkling halo . . .

'A seal!' he exclaimed. The creature dived. Ben swung the glasses in an arc, but found only slow ripples on the green swell of water. He lowered the binoculars, looked at the girl. 'Sorry, they've gone.'

'It's OK. I've been watching them for a while. I spotted them yesterday.' She took the glasses from him and looped the strap over her head again. 'I counted six full-grown, and four pups.' She pointed with her chin at the distant line of rocks. 'At low water those're islands. The seals'll come up on them soon.'

'Is that what you were looking for at the boat?' he asked. Before he remembered that it revealed that he'd seen her, that he'd been watching.

She glanced at him quizzically. He saw her eyes were very blue in a skinny brown face. Flushing, he explained, 'I stopped over there,' gesturing across the bay. He couldn't see the boat from here. 'The pack weighs a tonne . . .'

She said, 'Michael's place is on a bit more – over the next ridge.' Not answering his question. Adding, 'I'll help with the pack.' She moved round behind him and tugged it forcefully off his shoulders.

7

'Hey!' he protested.

'I'll take it down the easy bit – downhill all the way. You get it back for the climb.' She jerked it up, side-stepping with the sudden weight, grinned at him, and set off at an astonishing pace, already dipping out of sight in a hollow in the track.

Ben shrugged, found himself grinning too, and sprinted after her.

Two

She drifts, bumping the rock. Seaweed laces her legs and her hair spreads thin on the tide. She rolls with the wave, and her face rises to look at him.

Sea foam bubbles in her mouth.

She rolls, and her head twists in the grip of the rock, in the swirl of cold black water. He flounders, falls, stumbles, reaches for her—

Pale arms float wide, fingers weave the weed . . .

'Ben.'

The voice loud.

'*Ben.*'

He forces a face into focus. Beside him. Michael. Holding a mug.

Ben watches the mug lowered to the floor by the bed.

He is wringing with sweat, though the room is cool. He struggles to push the bleakness away. He can taste salt on his tongue.

Through the small window only the glare of a bright day.

'Are you OK?' Michael's voice again. He had retired to the doorway, propped against the jamb, his shoulders bulky in its low, crooked angles. 'You were thrashing about.'

'Sorry—A dream . . .' Though he was awake now, it filled him still, a cloying, drugging darkness.

Michael nodded. 'Take your time. Tea beside you. Have a shower, grab some breakfast. It's a good morning—' He had already disappeared, his voice receding through the neighbouring room, sunlight flooding in with the opening outer door. Suddenly the warmth looked and smelled good. Ben threw back the covers, picked up the tea and headed after his uncle. The shower, he remembered, was an outhouse on the end of the cottage.

Outside he paused, barefoot on dewy grass. The loch was creamed silver in the early light and Michael was on the shore. Beyond – a thread on shining water – something glided, entered sunlight and revealed itself as a canoe. Paddles arced in long, rhythmic strokes.

Michael waved. The paddles twirled an answer. Ben gulped tea, stretched, thought this must be as far from home in London as he could ever imagine. And hoped, glimpsing a boat's mast passing against the far shore, that today Michael would take him out there, as he'd promised in the letter, right out into the middle, on a boat. Wondered, too, if the girl would be somewhere on the loch, or the shore, or the bay.

In the shower he stood under peaty brown water, watched it spin down the drain and take the last of the shadowing gloom of the nightmare with it.

Though he did puzzle at the dream – why he'd had it, where it came from – unused as he was to such imaginings, good or bad.

They went to the boat, early, as soon as Ben had dressed and eaten, rattling in Michael's old van on the road that looped behind the headland to the bay.

They met only one other car. It appeared from behind and Michael moved aside on the narrow single-track road. Three cheery blasts of the horn and it was past and speeding on towards the ferry.

'Ferry-Bob,' volunteered Michael. 'He was ready to give you a lift down yesterday.'

'I know. I left a message with one of the ferrymen,' said Ben. 'I'd been sitting for four hours on the coach! I just wanted to walk.'

Michael nodded. 'Ferry-Bob dropped by to tell me.'

Ben digested this. At the ferry people had known who he was. So did the girl. Maybe everyone did. Maybe all the time he thought he was alone by the loch there'd been a bush-telegraph broadcasting his every move . . .

The van slowed to a halt. The bay was still shadowed blue by the hills, and for a moment he thought the boat had gone – till he found it in the blackness below the boulders. Nothing looked the same. It was low tide, the sandflats alive with strutting birds. There was a pool with a lone stalking heron and the boulder-ridge jutted far out, almost closing the mouth of the bay.

He scanned the crags for where he'd stood with the girl. Then waves had surged against the cliff below. Now just dry rock spilled from the base to the sudden teeth of a ragged spine. Thin streams meandered through the sand-channel between the headland rocks and the boulder-ridge. It was all that was left of the tide.

Abruptly Michael announced, 'It just came out of nowhere,' mysteriously, until Ben saw he was looking at the boat, and *that* was what he meant. 'It pelted down – rain day after day. And then hellish winds, even the ferry didn't run. I hate being cooped up – walked this way a fair bit. The morning after a really bad storm, there it was – reared up out of the sand. Strangest looking thing . . . I thought – *animal – dead seal or something*. But it was the bows, the rest still buried. Bit further out, of course: Ferry-Bob got the idea of digging it out and moving it up. Crazy . . . tides didn't get up that far again . . .'

The van swallowed the rest. He leaned in and grabbed a bag, tossed it at Ben, heaved up a second and slammed the door.

Ben caught the missile, heavier than expected, and nearly dropped it. 'Sorry – tools,' apologised Michael, and smiled. 'One of your mother's boat-repair books, too – I need a few tips and she sends a library!' Already he was moving down across slabs of rock to a green expanse that wasn't there yesterday. Submerged, Ben guessed, at high water.

He followed his uncle, slower, his trainers feeling large and unhelpful on the grooves of the rock. He was frustrated that Michael was already halfway to the boat before he'd squelched on to the soggy green plateau. It was grass, he discovered, sculpted by the tides into miniature islands and valleys. Water snaked below, hollowing and tunnelling so that suddenly (he found too soon) – an island might collapse and pitch him in water to the knees.

He pulled out one sodden foot and swore. He adjusted his grip on the toolbag and squinted at the best route to the boat.

Michael was taking a bit of getting used to. *Michael* was definitely not what he'd expected. His memories gave him a large man. Like the letters his uncle had written over the seven years in Canada: newsy, easy, *familiar . . .*

This Michael was smaller. Not really remarkable: *I'm fifteen now, not eight.* But this Michael was also thin – *older than I remember.* And this Michael talked all the time, peppering words with spurts of activity that took him away, out of earshot – like now, not finishing the story of the boat, or this morning, rushing down to the shore. Or yesterday. The first meeting awkward: letters not the same as face to face, in the flesh. But it wasn't that bad, because Michael swept him into a guided tour of the cottage and its grassy shelf below the pines. (Belongs to a friend – lived here for years, now he works in Glasgow . . .)

So how long are you staying? and *When're you going back to Canada?* was all Ben asked.

Iona's seals might be moving with the tide was the peculiar answer, and Michael bolting off for a scramble up the rocks before nightfall to see. Ben not realising till later, drifting to sleep, that Iona must be the girl.

Now, trailing his uncle, he made up his mind to stop being

13

baffled by it all. *E-ea-easy* . . . he mimicked Michael teaching him to climb the playground ropes. A long, long time ago. *E-ea-easy* . . .

He negotiated the last islands of sopping grass. On to sand: wet, but firm. Closer to the boat, he could see it was propped on heavy wooden struts. Birds darted upwards as he neared and something large slithered noisily on damp seaweed, flapped heavily away, zigzagged lazily across the shallows . . .

The boat is bigger than he expects. Broad-beamed and strong. Except for the hole in its flank.

He puts the bag down and steps closer. And for some reason he lays a hand flat on the wood, just as the girl did yesterday. It is warm and rough against his palm. He runs his fingers along the curve. It is streaked with traces of indistinct colour. He crouches and looks into the hole, and he thinks, *It's sad, it'll be good if we can mend it*, and wonders what the inside of the boat looks like.

He kneels down beside it. He pushes his head through the torn frame of the hole – and the chill flows over him like a breath exhaled; it swallows him, engulfs him, fills his mouth and his nose and his lungs so that he gasps and struggles for air and jerks back, his head shooting suddenly from the boat's cold gloom into sunlight: gulls lifting to the air – the bay loud with mewing cries, soft trills, distant harsher croaks.

He steadies himself and tries a tentative, new, deep breath. He smells only warm seaweed and the woodiness of the boat. But he hears her voice. The canoe is nosing into the shallows

14

and Michael catches the rope she throws. Iona crouches, rises, steps out of the canoe, shoulders the paddles. Michael hauls the craft to a dry berth above the tidemark.

Iona waggles a hand at Ben in greeting. She pulls herself up into the boat. She smiles down from her elevated perch. Michael is unsurprised by her arrival. Now that she is here, Ben is unsurprised too. She is expected, waited for.

'You coming up?' she wants to know. But she turns away and lets him clamber up in private, and he is impressed, surprised that he is up there beside her, rapidly and without mishap.

The boards are stained and blistered and they creak as he moves. But they are solid: the boat seems to float above the bay, and Ben feels tall and windswept and immensely free. He surveys the loch – to his right where the headland hides Michael's place; to his left where sheep graze the shore towards the distant ferry. Iona, who stands as she did yesterday, and doesn't hear him ask if she is looking for the seals.

From below comes Michael's voice. 'Move carefully, you two. Don't want you crashing through – broken bones and smashed wood to worry about.'

He smiles as he says it. It is only afterwards that Ben recalls how the smile falters. As if Michael is startled. And that for some time after that, Michael says nothing – as though there is something that absorbs him utterly, that excludes everything else . . .

Afterwards, though, looking back, Ben does remember. And in remembering, he understands.

Three

All morning they stayed with the boat. They learned its curves and angles and corners, poked about in its hidden places: scraped, pressed, tapped – checked for broken things, rusty metal, splintered wood, stubs of chalk ready to mark anything Michael needed to look at.

Iona settled to teaching Ben. She patted the rim of the boat, insisting '*gunwale*', or '*bows, stern*', when he called it front or back; '*keel*' – for the great wood spine of the boat – 'You can't work on a boat and not know the names!' But she said it without barb, and Ben teased, recited the names solemnly, mimicked her emphasis.

'Look for anything odd or different,' Michael instructed. 'Soggy patches, funny colour, mottles, spots, streaks, crusts, anything that *might* be mould or fungus . . .'

And then there was silence, comfortable and long, while under the hard blue dome of the sky the heat built steadily. Iona took the inside, probing the ribs and planking above the bottom boards. Then she went about tapping lightly all over the hull with a small hammer, because the book said that rotten wood sounded different.

Ben and Michael inspected the keel. 'Solid oak,' said Michael, and knocked it with his knuckle. He was squatting down, and now he put his head in the dark hole just as Ben had done. For a gasp of a moment there was a fluttering expectation in Ben, a flicker of cold premonition. But then Michael stood up, went over to the toolbag, unzipped it, pulled out a book – and the moment was gone.

With his back to the sun, shirt off and draped over his head, Michael sat cross-legged. He propped the volume open on the bag. Suddenly his square, freckled back was very familiar to Ben, memories surfacing sharply – of being small and clambering to his shoulders to be carried. And he felt a surge of elation at being here, as he'd felt on the ferry yesterday: he was leaving the real world behind with the receding land and crossing to something altogether special, altogether different.

He looked up at Iona. She smiled down at him. She moved forward to that place she seemed to like to stand, in the stern of the boat. And she was suddenly quite still: as if listening. As if *hearing*.

Again the coldness flooded Ben, gone again in a moment, so fast he wondered if he'd imagined it, or if the sun was making him weird – ill. He was unaccountably anxious and took a step towards her. Her gaze passed across him. But she didn't see him. She looked back into the boat. Then she swung her legs over the side and dropped down. She walked rapidly away, frowning.

He pushed the hair off his forehead in frustration. Too hot.

17

Thirsty. His head ached with the glare, a terrible restlessness came over him. He had to do something to erase this peculiar darkening unease.

He went and looked over Michael's shoulder at the page he was reading.

SOFT ROTS. These erode from the surface down, rendering the top layers wet and soft, sometimes powdery . . . Dried out, it leaves surface cracks . . .

There were pictures of mottled colours, wood grain raised and split. Almost pretty.

'There's nothing like that,' he remarked, interested.

Michael grunted. He flipped a page over. 'Look at this . . .' Wood riddled with tiny holes. 'A keel just like ours,' he explained. 'But with gribbles in it. They bore in . . .'

He got to his feet and carried the book to the boat. Ben followed. They held the picture against the keel and Michael ran his fingers across the wood, scratched lightly, shook his head.

Ben lowered himself to the sand and lay under the boat to examine it from that angle. No gribbles. *Good.* Why did Michael shake his head?

He rolled out from underneath and wished there was a breeze. Sweat ran in the hollows of his back and he didn't want to leave the shade below the boat. Water had begun to seep past the boulder-ridge and up the channel towards the heron's pool. With languid wingbeats the great bird rose to the air, circled, glided down to the ridge, turned its back on them.

Iona was paddling in the incoming surf. He could see her splash her face and damp back her hair. He wanted to be there too, to cool his legs, douse his hot face, this effort of the boat suddenly too much, too heavy, a load he wanted to put down, push away.

Wading birds made noisy protest at his approach, settled again, ignored him.

Iona looked up. She smiled. He threw water over his face and head. Birds fluttered upwards at the splashing and a trio set off in a frantic wheeling flight, scolding. Then Ben found himself laughing, as if his mood winged upwards with them.

Oystercatchers, Iona said, resuming lessons and pointing to others like them (black silhouettes on the sand; long, fine beaks). *Wagtails* (pied black and white twitching tails up and down). And the small brown ones like sparrows, cheeping shrilly? *Rock pipits*. (Does she know the names of every one?) Cormorants ranged in a silent dark army behind the heron, waiting for the tide.

On the beach Michael strolled towards the van. The boat stood alone, shadow lengthening the hole. It really would be good to mend it, Ben thought. *Like healing a wound*, the words coming to him with force.

With Iona he walked back up the sands towards it, through rafts of seaweed drifting in on the gathering tide.

Four

By midday, thirst and hunger drove them to the pub by the ferry. There was a traffic jam: three cars pulled off the little ferry's clanking metal ramp. A bus and a string of bicycles on the road vied for right-of-way and blocked the steep concrete slipway. A ferryman marched to direct operations.

Ben leaned with Iona against the seawall. The ferry reloaded. Five cars, an ambulance, two vans. They rolled down the slip, edged up the ramp and were beckoned into place. People left the vehicles and went to the rails to look across the water. Chains rattled, the winch groaned and hauled up the ramp; the ferry swung away.

Michael went in search of drinks and sandwiches, and came back with Ferry-Bob.

Ferry-Bob was a surprise.

Ben had pictured a large, muscular man. In big boots like a fisherman. Because of the tale of digging out the boat, maybe. Or the name.

But a small, spare figure grinned up at him from under a startling thatch of rusty hair. Thin and bony. Age impossible to guess: older than Michael. Or maybe just seamed by squinting at the wind. Baggy trousers and a faded leather satchel.

For only Iona to hear, Ben whispered, 'Why *Ferry*-Bob?'

Sharp-eared, Ferry-Bob raised his glass in salute. 'We-ell, there's a fair question, young Ben.' He mopped a damp forehead with his sleeve and took a sandwich from Michael's plate. 'My cousin Bob's to blame – at the fish farm yonder. He's always been here, mind, so he's a right to be Bob.' He chewed and winked. 'I'm the new one – so I'm Ferry-Bob, and there's no cause for a muddle.'

'New!' snorted Michael. 'Ten years – and from just down the coast before! He works on the ferry,' he added, stating the obvious. 5375/101.

Ferry-Bob patted the satchel. 'I'm on tickets in a minute. I'll just have this bit o' lunch and Andy down there'll do the run, and then I'll be on till she stops in the night.' He brandished the half-eaten sandwich at the sky, the loch, the mountains. He beamed at Ben. 'I reckon maybe you've brought all this.' Nodding. 'I reckon, young Ben, you're maybe good luck. Rain fit to drown us all and then this lad from London's here, and now it's the tropics!'

Ben grinned back at him. The water glittered and a breeze stirred round them, died lazily. He thought of the rucksack of warm clothes and rain gear his mother insisted he bring. Difficult to imagine *ever* needing it. Difficult to recall the mists of yesterday or rain spattering coach windows on the drive from Glasgow.

Ferry-Bob was saying to Michael, 'I got away down the fish farm, last evening. Like I said, found some heavy bits – good solid timber it is, but they've no use for it. I'll be round tomorrow to bring it . . .'

Tall tan sails entered the neck of the Narrows, moved to the centre of the quickening tide and travelled towards them. Iona nudged Ben. They watched idly. She nudged him again and pointed. 'The eagles,' she said. He followed the line of her finger, but saw only the green curtain of hills across the loch and then she'd slipped off the wall before he could ask *Where?* – going towards the cars queuing for the next ferry. He hoped she was coming back.

'So, do these books say anything? Are y'any the wiser?' Ferry-Bob was asking.

Michael shook his head. 'Maybe I'm being stupid, Ferry-Bob; maybe we're looking for the wrong things. There's lots about soft rot, you see: the books all say you'd expect it on wrecks that've been on the sea-bed for a long time. But that boat's got no rot. No decay. No gribbles. Not much damage, even. Just that hole . . .'

'Rocks,' said Ferry-Bob. 'It's a rock makes a hole like that.'

'Everything else is solid. *Sound*,' asserted Michael.

'We looked all over,' agreed Ben.

Ferry-Bob frowned. 'Maybe it's been in sand all the time – that's known to preserve wood in a fine way.' He took another sandwich. 'I reckon – if you're right, mind – I reckon there's a fair chance it's been buried in that sand awhile, maybe since it went down. It's the water and the oxygen does the harm.'

The tan sails were nearing the ferry's path. There were three great masts; the boat rose and fell on the green swell of the loch and seemed to sail straight out of some swashbuckling pirate film.

'Is it a fishing boat?' Ben asked. Meaning their own boat with its sad hole, not the glamorous thing that rode the Narrows towards them.

Michael shrugged. Ferry-Bob shook his head. 'Not like any fishing boat I know. Could be from anywhere, mind, pushed along by the tides. There's fair storms hereabouts.'

The tan sails were being hauled down. People scurried about on deck, voices shrilling across water. You could hear the engine.

'There's Annie,' said Michael, who hadn't looked at the ship but instead watched Iona talk to someone in a car. He raised a hand, and there was an answering gesture through the car window. For Ben's benefit he added, 'Iona's mother,' and Ben had a look, but couldn't see.

The ship was gliding past. Passengers on the returning ferry watched as it passed and people waved to each other from each deck.

'An expedition from the sailing school up the loch,' said Ferry-Bob. He punched Michael lightly on the arm, 'You'll be taking Ben out one of these days, then, Michael?'

Silence.

Then, 'No boat,' Michael murmured.

Ben looked at him. Michael didn't look at Ben.

Ben wanted to say in frustration, *you promised*, you wrote that we'd borrow or hire one. But he held back, hearing its petulance, not wanting to sound like his brother Joey, five years old and sulky when thwarted.

So I didn't imagine it yesterday. He *is* avoiding it.

Ferry-Bob saw his face and winked. 'It's his shabby excuse to get you slaving on that old wreck, Ben. Obsessions, Ben – obsessions . . .' He winked again. 'He *tells* me he teaches boating – "water skills" he calls it – on some big lake in Canada. But we never see him on *our* waters—'

Michael smiled at the dig. But there was no offer to take Ben out there, and now Ben knew there wasn't going to be one.

'My mother's off across.' Iona straddled the wall beside Ben. 'To Inverness – to fetch stuff . . .'

'She'll be hard-pushed to get the last ferry back,' observed Michael.

'Och, she'll drive round the head of the loch, or stay over with my Auntie till morning.'

Three canoes and a small red inflatable boat travelled in convoy across the foaming wake of the ferry. Ben saw Michael watch them. They tossed about, spun a little, drifted sideways. Suddenly Michael became very busy gathering up glasses and crossing the road to the pub.

Iona watched the boats too. She asked Ben, 'Have you ever canoed?'

'Once.' Should he say in a swimming pool and the canoe

capsized? 'I—'

She interrupted, 'I'll bring *Ulaidh*. *Tapuru* turns over too easy. You have to know her. *Ulaidh*'s heavier. She sits steady. We'll go two-up to the old lighthouse.'

Ulaidh. Tapuru. Canoes. He thought, I'm getting faster at this.

'There y'are,' announced Ferry-Bob. 'Canoe, loch, clever lass who knows what she's doing out there – y'r problem's all gone, Ben lad.'

To Iona Ben explained, 'I was hoping Michael'd teach me to sail. He offered . . .'

She pulled a face, which meant nothing to him.

He let the matter drop. And he wondered if her promise would be as short-lived as Michael's. Then he was annoyed with himself for the lingering, unreasonable, puzzled sense of something lost.

It was in the evening, still working on the boat, that he first noticed the woman. She stood near the van and seemed to have been there for some time.

There was no sign of where she'd come from. Odd, in this place where he could see no houses and only two or three cars passing the whole afternoon – and those only after a ferry docked. He could tell that now because he knew the thump of the ramp on the slip – you could hear it when the wind was right.

But then he thought, Iona wanders about, and Michael, so perhaps it's not so odd.

They packed up the tools, climbed towards the road and the van, and the woman watched them. Her clothes were a splash of bright yellow against the hill-slope. She stood very still and did not hide that she was looking at them.

Ben asked, 'Who's that?'

'Her croft's in the back field,' Michael said. 'Kelda,' he greeted her, reaching the road. She was very tall and very straight and very old.

'Michael,' she answered. Her voice unexpectedly soft. 'This'll be your nephew, then.'

'Ben,' agreed Michael.

She nodded at Ben, and gave him a long, direct look. And then she looked away, across the bay. It was not unfriendly. It was just that she was already saying, 'You're going to do it, then.'

'We'll have a go,' said Michael.

They're talking about the boat. Suddenly Ben was tired of all these sideways conversations, a festering exasperation he'd nursed since they'd returned from the ferry erupted, so that he wanted to get away, not have to listen or decipher any more.

He turned towards the headland. Iona was still in sight. Or rather the long shape of the departing canoe was, moving into shadow in that moment.

He went to the van. Michael and Kelda were still talking – except that he saw it was Michael who spoke and she who stood and listened. Then she crossed the road and walked slowly through the trees, and Ben saw the low white contours of her cottage, so tucked away you would miss it unless you traced the line of the track through the birch copse that rimmed the hill.

'I think she was standing there for a long time,' he said to Michael, driving back.

'She often does.'

'Do you think she minds? Us being in the bay?'

His uncle shook his head. 'She's curious, that's all. About the boat, I mean. I *think* she's curious . . .'

'Does she know anything about it?' Ben persisted, 'Did you ask her?'

'Didn't get an answer. Don't think she knows . . . Dunno – maybe she does.'

Ben was on the point of saying, *I s'pose it would be strange, living there, seeing the boat, wondering.* But then it was a thought he didn't want to complete and he let it alone and sat in silence till they reached the cottage.

But when he woke in the night from a dream, it was the woman's tall figure he'd been seeing, and her sunny yellow dress. Yet in the dream she was not standing on grass beside a road below a hill. She was on a pier, and behind her a jumble of houses; she was waving and he knew her, spoke to her; she laughed, and he laughed, but then she was crying, and she was not the woman Kelda but Iona, and he woke then and it was all he remembered of a dream that left him limp with sweat and kept him from sleeping till the first pale daylight lifted the darkness in his room.

Five

Yet it is not the dreams that linger in his mind afterwards – in the long waiting time that follows. It is the sound and smell and colour of those days that burns in his memory. The play of light on water: silver, turquoise, gold. The peaks of an endless purple landscape that folds away on either side. The peculiar echoing silence of the loch on windless mornings: a child's voice piping on the shore, the plop of a fish, the silvery trickle of a bird dipping, shaking, diving . . .

Other times, too, with the tide running swift and a sharp breeze ruffling the water, when the seals come and swim in wide circles about them and look with their round, dark eyes. And he feels something indescribable that he cannot voice even to Iona. He sees now why she shares hours with them, riding the waters silently in *Ulaidh*.

The water-sound is a hollow slapslap; the wind a talkative rustle in their ears. The seals dive and return, dive and return, trailing the canoe to the boundaries of their territory.

Ulaidh is their home. His first cautious efforts in the canoe transform through Iona's teaching to a natural ease: he is good at it, he finds – learning the paddle-strokes rapidly, matching the cadence she sets in a partnership soon effortless.

Sometimes they hug the coast. They follow water that pushes between rocks, carves gorges, hollows echoing caves. They nose the canoe in on slack water, fasten it and climb, survey their kingdom from the heights.

They stay well away when the tide swells over the rocks and masks the sharpness below.

They swim in water that makes him gasp – so cold, so green; land on stony beaches among yellow flowers; follow sheep tracks through heather to open hills. Deer graze the tops and eye them watchfully.

From outcrops of rock Iona makes him look for the circling eagles of the higher glen. 'There's two pairs, one here and one in the glen behind the ferry – they were flying the other day . . .' (She'd pointed at them and he'd failed to see.)

At first he can't spot the soaring specks – so high against the mountains they must be enormous for anyone to see with a naked eye. Distances across these tracts of wild land confuse him, familiar only with the chopped-up contours of city views. And the look of the land from the water astonishes him. Distances narrow or widen with the ebb and flow of tides. Rock, bay, forest, valley merge to a hazy rim and he cannot tell if the shore is ten miles away or a short pull in the canoe. Then they paddle closer and the land breaks into surprise islands, or the fist of a single promontory splits to two or three with beaches, craggy tree-slopes, meadows and grazing sheep between.

And the biggest surprise of all – that the loch he sees from Michael's place and the loch he sees from the boat's bay are not the same.

Ben hadn't understood that, and he felt stupid, realising it. He did not want Iona to know his mistake. He resolved to find a map and have a proper look.

But his reluctance to reveal his muddle evaporated because he knew she never minded how little he knew, never made a thing of it.

She constructed a map on the rock with strands of seaweed, coloured pebbles and shells from the beach.

'You'll have to learn it,' she said, 'or you'll go out on the water one day and never come home!'

She heaved a glossy black boulder to mark the headland. Pink and grey pebbles were the boulders round the boat's bay. Seaweed curved away to north-east and south-west to form the main sea loch with the ferry at its elbow and its opening to the sea at its southernmost end.

But then Iona showed that (tucked in behind the headland, out of sight if you looked at it from the boat) the water pushed in to make another, smaller loch. It wriggled sideways to the west before curving northwards between low hills – *opening off* the main sea loch.

'There's Michael's cottage,' she said, and placed a mottled pebble on the smaller loch's north-eastern shore.

'See, the headland looks left to the boat in the bay, forward to the big sea loch – here're the seal islands,' (dropping shells across the seaweed 'loch' to show them). 'But on the right and at the back, it looks down at Michael's cottage – on the *little* loch.'

Ben studied the shapes she made. So different from the picture he'd carried. At the time, sitting beside Iona, it was just that he wanted to know this place, to really *see* this world of hers.

Only much later – in the remembrance of that day – would meanings stir in his mind. From where they were sitting, the headland was visible across the water, low tide baring great slabs of rock at its base. Cormorants crowned the strange ridge at the outer edge – darker, different, as if a giant hand had taken a slab and tipped it up to make a jagged wall fine-seamed with blackened rock. It lined one side of the entrance to the smaller loch.

As he watched, a cormorant dropped to the waves and floated there. Then with slow wingbeat and long black neck outstretched, it rose to skimming flight across the loch, swerved wide and came towards them, alighting in the shade beside *Ulaidh*. The canoe lay on the shore below them, here on *Rudha Dhubh*. Black Point, the name meant, Iona'd told him on their first venture to this finger of bare rock. From this side of the smaller loch it stabbed out sharply, pointing straight across the water – towards the headland rising opposite. He saw now that *Rudha Dhubh* was the other edge of the entrance to the smaller loch.

At high tide deep water lapped its shores. Only the ebb tide revealed the stony causeway to the islets further out – each a miniature land of mountain, valley, forest, cliff and bay – just big enough to walk round in five minutes, each ringed by water at high tide. All linked by the hidden reef to this rocky shore.

Rudha Dhubh had become – Ben thought of it as – their place.

'You can't get here, except by boat,' Iona said. 'There's no road this side.' She pointed to the granite crags behind them. 'Over there are hills and glens and then you come down again to the big loch, which is going away to the sea.'

Ben looked again at the shapes on her map. Then up at the real waters before him. With the turning tide, the current flowed fast and powerful into the smaller loch – a rushing, turbulent race through the deep channel that cut the last islet on this side from the bare lower slabs of the headland on the other. But in a few hours there would be only a wide sweep of glinting water, hiding all.

Iona dropped a large white shell on her map. 'Here's the old lighthouse.' It rose to their left – and it had no light. Just a chipped pillar of stone high on a bluff, topped by an empty platform, and below that a small chamber that once housed the machinery for the light. Now it was open to the winds and cormorants and nesting gulls. 'And here . . .' she traced a line on her map beyond the derelict pillar towards the head of the smaller loch, '. . . round the bend of the little loch, but over on the opposite shore (you can't see it from here), that's where you'll find the Old Village. You get to it on the road past Michael's place.'

That was something else he'd wondered about, for he'd not seen it yet. And he'd been puzzled by the way it was called the Old Village, but he'd met no one here who actually lived there, all coming instead from the cluster of houses round the ferry and its busy pub, way up on the shores of the main sea loch.

He did see the Old Village later that day, paddling towards it in *Ulaidh* – a straggle of cottages along the ledge of a road that cut across the hills, dipped to the shore, rose again to the cliff at the head of the loch. At once he thought, *I've seen this before.* But he hadn't, couldn't – had never driven there with Michael, never gone up the smaller loch beyond his uncle's cottage.

It came to him then, with a jolt of recognition: they were the jumbled houses of his dream – the woman Kelda stood before them in her yellow dress, laughed and waved at him . . .

But there was no pier here, and she'd been standing on a pier; he could never have seen this place before, and the strangeness of it worried him. He wanted to tell Iona. Then he was afraid to and did not know why and tried instead to push it from his mind.

He looked at the cliff. A large house sat squarely on the top. He had seen that before – a pale shape glinting sometimes with the play of sunlight on it. You could just see it from *Rudha Dhubh*.

'Shallachain House, where I live now,' Iona told him. 'It's a ruin that they're making into a hotel. My mother's "general manager" – *dogsbody* she is really – runs about for this and that and the owner flies in from fancy places and gives orders.' She pulled down the corners of her mouth and sniffed, and Ben laughed at the look of her face, burying his unease.

He could see the house clearly. Square and pale on the red-brown cliff-top. Set apart, above the last houses of the village. Its squareness was uneven – as if some of the roof was missing.

'From the fire,' explained Iona. 'Years and years ago . . .'

They landed at the base of the cliff. The narrow beach was strewn with boulders and slippery with seaweed. She led him up the path to the house. It was steep and dusty and wound to and fro between great bulges of rock. Trees grew at unlikely angles. Heather clung to mossy ledges. 'Terrible in the wet,' she said. 'You can't use it, you slide straight off. OK now it's dry.'

But they slithered on loose sand, grabbed handholds on rocks and tree roots, puffed and gasped at the steepness, sat for a while halfway, and Ben had a twinge of shock when he looked down and saw how high they'd come.

They pushed through bracken to a sloping lawn below the house. The skeleton of roofbeams showed. Plastic sheeting flapped. He saw the fire-blackening of timbers. Large windows, empty of glass, looked out at them.

On the other side there was the buzz of vans manœuvring, heaps of builders' sand, pallets of wood, stacks of brick, a general thumping and banging, loads carried to and fro, the whirr and grind of electric saws, shouting from someone on a ladder doing something to a high window and someone else passing below.

There were nods of greeting as they went past, and in a large kitchen smelling of damp new plaster, cups of tea were handed out and Iona's mother stood talking. They sat about eating biscuits till she was finished.

Meeting her, Ben was somehow surprised. Iona called her Annie, not Mum or Ma, or Mother, or Mam, or anything he expected. And she was a larger, plumper version of Iona, the hair tamer and shorter, the face rounder, but the same characteristic waggle of the hand in greeting, the same quick, light voice, the same blue eyes, direct and questioning. And he had the sensation of having seen her before, though he knew he had not, just as he could not have seen the Old Village or known Kelda before.

Mad! he told himself fiercely. *Ridiculous – brain short-circuiting. Tricks. Like the weird dreams.* He worked harder at looking around, asking questions, forcing the feeling away.

'Tell about the fire,' he said to Iona.

'House burned down. In the middle of the night – *and* the owner disappeared,' she answered.

'*And* there's all kinds of stories about it,' added someone passing by, hearing his question. 'But no one really knows.'

And so the feeling did go. There was too much noise and scurrying about, too many people talking to Iona, too much she wanted him to see in the great house powdered with building dust but still grand – high-ceilinged rooms, long windows, the graceful spiralling staircase that was its particular pride.

'The *original* owner liked to have the latest of everything. Had that made up and shipped up here, would you believe!' said Annie.

But she too was only moving past then, friendly but distracted, rushing away soon, harassed at the bleep of a mobile phone. She did not appear again before they left – after Iona took him round the outside of the house, and they'd peered in behind plastic curtains at the great front room, once a ballroom, she said, filled now with ladders and boards.

There was also the back wing, smaller, with its own entrance, where she and Annie had lived for the past few months.

'The old servants' quarters. It was the laird's house once, or his son's – can't remember, really. Until it burned, that is . . .'

And after that, when they left, Ben thought no more about Shallachain House, except to store it in his mind as the place where Iona came from each morning in *Ulaidh*.

Six

'I might have known!' he said to her later, laughing.

She had a particular purpose in taking him there. He discovered it next morning when she called him from the shore at Michael's place.

A small white bucket of a boat sat on the shingles. Yellow sails fluttered in the breeze. Iona beamed with the pleasure of her surprise.

'*Findhorn*. Annie let me borrow her from the house. She says you look a *sensible* lad,' and she grinned happily.

So then there were sailing lessons after all. She put him in charge of the daggerboard first. He had to lower it through a slot in the hull in deep water but pull it up fast when they came in shallow. Then he had a chance on the tiller – to feel *Findhorn*'s shift as he pushed it one way or the other and moved the rudder through the water.

At first the little boat heeled wildly: he was moving the tiller too far, too fast, and it needed a subtle touch. But he began to understand it, and the handling of the ropes that she called sheets, for controlling the sail. He learned to stop the boat dead – letting everything go and spilling the wind; to feel the tug and lean of the boat when he pulled the sails taut, hear the hollow flap when he let them loose.

He began to know the wind a little better, see its capricious change of mood, its treachery Iona always warned him about . . .

So that, between *Ulaidh* when the wind was slack and *Findhorn* when the breeze was up, they stayed out later and later, till the low sun reddened the hills and they darted in and out of tongues of shadow to where she left him, each evening, on Michael's shore.

Yet still they circled at some time each day, like homing birds, to the bay, and the work on the boat, and to Michael.

At the beginning they had asked him to come with them on the water – an expedition with both canoes along the loch.

He refused. They stopped asking.

He fussed about lifejackets. Too often he asked Ben if he was a strong swimmer. The repeated question began to exasperate. *Swimming* Ben was good at – his uncle knew, he was in the school team. He was puzzled why Michael seemed not to believe, seemed not to *want* to believe. On the boats they did always wear lifejackets, too. Iona demonstrated, throwing the canoe into a capsize, tipping them both in the water, showing they could right it and get in quickly, that they knew what they were doing.

Then Michael had a good look at *Ulaidh*, checked the hull,

the paddles, watched them circle the bay several times, till the frustration of it infuriated Ben and, just in time, Michael was satisfied and waved them off.

He would not join them, though; Ben and Iona nagged and even Ferry-Bob urged.

Ferry-Bob had come with a letter for Michael. It had arrived at the pub.

Michael took it, didn't look at it, put it away in his pocket.

Ferry-Bob shook his head in mock amazement. 'Y'r uncle's a dark horse, Ben, and that's a fact . . .' he said. But there was something other than amusement in his tone and Ben saw him eyeing Michael with a frown.

Michael was intent only on plans to repair the hole in the boat. He sat in the long evenings outside the cottage, light fading over the mountains, leafing through books, talking to Ferry-Bob.

'Och, let's just have a go,' said Ferry-Bob, 'We'll go slow and look careful. There's no cause for worry, Michael . . .'

But how to prop the hull safely while they took out damaged planks? Where to cut back into sound wood?

Ferry-Bob brought the timber from the fish farm that he'd promised. They all helped to fashion the cradle to hold the boat, testing its angles and fixings, putting it in place round the boat, piece by piece.

There was scraping and sanding and cleaning. Michael made lists of glues and varnishes to buy. He went off with Ferry-Bob in search of good strong nails . . .

Seven

These are the good memories. They have the colour of warmth. They are threaded with the memories of Iona – as she was, as Ben wants her to be . . .

He has other memories of the boat. Fragmented. Savage. Like the moments themselves.

Fury – from nowhere. It pierces him like a stab of pain, and he does not know why, there is no meaning or reason to it, he has never felt this before and it terrifies him.

Sudden silences – they follow the fury, wash over the boat, hang like a curtain of gloom. Iona goes away without speaking and the day takes on a bleakness.

It clings round them till her reappearance the next day erases it.

Yet the day comes when the boat's cradle is finished. Ferry-Bob is there to help.

Michael begins to saw. The first splintered wood from the edge of the hole lies on the sand.

Ben stoops and picks up a fragment. He turns it in his hand.

It feels heavy, warm from the friction of the saw. It has the clean, fragrant smell of cut wood.

He turns it over.

He knows it the moment he sees it, there for him to see, there, burned on the other side, burned on the plank, burned for his eyes . . .

The name: the boat's name.

Sea Hawk.

It was that day, too, that Iona stopped coming to the boat.

PART TWO
IONA

Eight

She drifts, bumping the rock. She lifts on the wave and her face turns to him – bleak face, bleak eyes . . .

He slips, slides on the wet rock and falls to the pool and she lurches, rolls – rolls to his face, he is trapped, wrapped, bound in the wet dark swirl of her skirts—

Blackness. Pillow smothering. Sticky. Damp against his mouth.

Darkness thick with heat.

Light filtered beneath the door. With the sweat of his palm, the handle slipped in his grip.

The outer door was open.

Outside there was fitful moonlight, banks of slow-moving cloud. Michael's shape was dark against the paler wash of the loch. He turned at Ben's approach.

'Can't sleep? Hot, isn't it?'

Ben wanted to say, 'It's this dream . . .' But he didn't. They stood together, catching the slight breeze off the water.

Ben said in a rush, 'Why did Iona run off this afternoon? Did she say anything?'

He'd gone to the toolbag to fetch nails. When he'd turned back she was already in *Ulaidh*, paddling fast.

He'd asked, 'Has she gone?' Fretting already at Michael's closed-up mouth. They'd packed up then in silence, returned home . . .

In the darkness now Michael shrugged off the question. 'Don't let it worry you, Ben. People have their moments . . .'

'But did someone say something to her?' Meaning, *did you say something* – no one else was there.

But Ben knew: there'd have been that look on Iona's face. Even from here he felt its coldness – like the breath from the boat, he had it still – a smell of misery stalking him from the first day.

Like the smell of his dreams.

In bed he stared at the pale square of the window, looking for the dawn. He was not surprised when she did not come to the shore for him in the morning.

Gone was the hard, dry heat. Clouds rimmed the mountains to the west, massing dark and heavy but holding off their cargo of rain.

He woke late, startled out of sleep by some uneasy knowledge from another dream he could not remember, and by the silence in the cottage.

He went to the shore, hoping for Iona. There was only Michael, and a carnage of jellyfish, like a delicate mauve necklace across the whites and greys and browns of the shingles.

'Are they all dead?' he asked in horror.

'I think so.' Michael lifted one gently on a piece of driftwood and floated it into the shallows. It hung limp, swished back by the next ripple of surf. It lay there again.

'Never seen anything like it. They're the whole length of the shore. Washed in by the tide and stranded, I s'pose.' Michael shook his head.

They were on the boat's bay too, strung at the highwater mark across the mounds of drying weed. Midges rose in agitated clouds. There was a curious silence. No birds; the air humid with a dulling warmth.

They stood for a moment and gazed at the forlorn sight. Michael turned several lifeless, transparent shapes with his foot. Then he stepped across them and went on towards the boat.

Ben watched his uncle walking away. There was an obscure desolation in watching him, in feeling again his absorption with the boat, in knowing there would be another failed conversation about Iona, Ben not really saying, Michael not really listening, not really *wanting* to listen, dismissing everything as some kind of adolescent mood in Iona − her boredom with them and with the boat.

Was it? *Was it?*

Why had Iona stopped coming? The day without her stretched away with an unexpected blankness. There'd been no day without her since he'd got here.

He gazed across the loch. *If I look long enough I'll see her coming past the headland.*

Yet even in that first hour of her absence that morning, he knew he would not.

He pulls his mind back from Iona to here, to now. It needs effort, as if hauling himself up through a saturating numbness – cold, wet, drowning him like iced water.

Today it's the broken hull to be worked on. Michael plans to make his first cut into the damaged wood. He is restless to start.

Suddenly so is Ben. Suddenly he hates the barrenness of the boat marooned with the dead jellyfish on this shore.

The hole looms closer, shadow like a spreading stain.

Fill it, mend it, *heal the wound.*

MY WOUND *MY* LIFE *MINE!*

Blood pounds in his head. The words drum with the blood. The boat undulates through the blurring in his eyes, Michael's figure flickers in the blur.

This is *crazy*. I'm going mad. No sleep: too hot . . .

It's OK, OK – Ferry-Bob's car-door slamming, Ferry-Bob's sharp, quick figure crossing the beach.

He fights for breath. He can hear the rasp of Michael's first slow saw-stroke . . .

The wood with the name *Sea Hawk* is in his hand. Michael takes it from him and turns it over. 'Maybe they put that somewhere inside in case they were wrecked.'

Ferry-Bob comes and looks and grunts. 'Ben here should keep it safe for us. We'll maybe put it back – when we're done, eh, Michael?'

Ben takes the wood to the toolbag, props it up.

She should see it. She should be here. It is the same fury hurtling upwards, gone again even as he grapples to push it down, outlandish, alien, washed then by the silence, like the slow, cold ebb of a tide.

In the afternoon he went searching, scrambling down from rock to rock on the headland trying to see their place on *Rudha Dhubh* across the loch.

He couldn't. The distant shore was no more than a pale brown fringe in the haze. No seals moving either. Only the heron stood sentinel on the boulder-ridge in the bay, beyond the shadow of the boat called *Sea Hawk*.

And Kelda's still figure, waiting, below the hill.

Nine

The flame snakes from his hand, hissing, flares yellow . . .

. . . yellow-red, yellow in the blackness, yellow tongue . . .

. . . wet salt wetness on my face, she goes away through the black into the yellow . . .

. . . bright stars in the black . . .

. . . No! Not me . . .

MY LIFE!

MINE!

Covers on the floor. Drag them up, but then he is hot, not with the heat of the night, with the heat of the fire that flares behind eyelids.

Light licks below the door.

Michael . . .

He lies watching the light, keeps it before him, dreads sleep . . .

Scorching . . . flames . . .

Coiling . . .

. . . red . . . snakes . . .
. . . blood . . . blood . . .
. . . cold . . . cold . . .

Awake. Face in the pillow. Block out the blackness the brightness the sounds . . .

. . . red . . . blood . . .
 . . . coiling . . .
 No . . . she—

Morning. The stench of smoke sharp in his nostrils. Eyes burn. Memories beckon: the hiss and bellow of a furnace, but not the coiling flame of the dream, the yellow snake in the dark – it is a cupboard with a door and the burn is good, bright, warm, there is laughter and the voice of a girl he turns to greet, her quick, light footsteps . . .

. . . but it is only Ferry-Bob coming into the cottage, and the laugh is only the laugh of his wild imagination – Iona's laugh, he thinks, a memory, or a hope, or a wish.

'I have to go on up to Shallachain House,' Ferry-Bob had come to say. 'You'll be wanting to come?'

For the second day she had not appeared at the shore or the boat.

Over breakfast he'd tried to talk to Michael. It was the half-conversation he feared, Michael brightly brushing off the attempt, talking only of plans for the day, Ben lapsing to silence. Angry at his own limpness. Trapped in it. Miserable helplessness. How to *tell it*? How to tell his uncle about the dreams? About this shifting unease.

He'd had a friend who kept trying to tell people about dreams. No one wanted to listen – *I* didn't want to listen. Can't take it seriously!

What to say now? How to make sense of it? Why this nebulous, nagging worry?

He'd thought back over the times Iona'd gone away before. The sudden closing of her face. Sometimes she just seemed to be somewhere else in her thoughts: bored.

Maybe it *was* just boredom.

But she'd always come back again, the next day, as if nothing had happened.

Maybe, he thought, if I find her at the house it'll be as if nothing has happened.

What has happened?

Ferry-Bob drove slowly, stopping for the languid passage of sheep across the road, glancing sideways at Ben.

'She's just off for a day or two, no doubt. Don't let it get you down, Ben lad. There's other things she wants to do – probably. She'll be somewhere about – and then she'll just turn up. We'd hear if anything was wrong.'

'I'm not—'

Ben didn't finish the protest. What wasn't he?

He wanted her to be there. He did not want her not to be. He was scared that she was not. He could not say why. He could not say any of it. There was no logic to it – it was an inexpressible wavering nervousness – like a nudging urgency, a waiting for something to happen and a dread that it would.

They were passing the old Village. A few people walked in front of cottages. Three women talking. An old man with a dog. They stopped and turned and looked at the car. They looked at Ben.

Ferry-Bob slowed, stopped beside the old man, wound down his window.

'Calum,' he called, 'are you all right, man?'

'I am,' was the answer. The man was looking past Ferry-Bob, at Ben. It was a direct, steady, curious stare. He said nothing else.

'And Jeannie?' pressed Ferry-Bob.

Calum turned his head and looked along the road to where the women stood together. They'd also stopped, and now they were watching Calum and the car.

'Jeannie's fine,' Calum said. 'We'll do. We'll all do.' He nodded briefly, nudged the dog, began to walk on, slow and stiff in his movements.

Ben thought, they're *old*, like Kelda – there isn't anyone young round here.

He said it to Ferry-Bob. To prove him wrong, two children ran towards the sands and a small brown dog began to chase them, yapping. Behind, there strolled an older boy, skimming pebbles at the waves.

'Visitors, they'll be,' said Ferry-Bob, noting Ben's gaze on them.

'How d'you know?'

'Oh, I know. They'll be from the holiday cottages. There's two at the end of the village. See, the young local families don't live up here, they're down at the ferry stop – the new houses beyond the ferry pub and the garage.' As an afterthought he added, 'They don't want to be up here. People stay here – some stay on till they die – there's been a few of the old ones died this past year or two. But no one *new* comes in.'

There's something dark about this place, Ben thought. But then – the dark is in me, not in the place, and at the same time he thought *it's in both* – and it brought a rush of raw fear. He shifted uneasily in the seat. But he said nothing. He thought, I'm just depressed. People *do* get depressed.

But not like this – not me, not me before, never like this.

' 'Course it's easier up the other end,' Ferry-Bob was saying. 'Close to the ferry – they can get across easy – school's on the other side. Bit dismal up here – odd, really. Some o' the old ones've been here all their lives, you'll not find them going away any place else. Calum and Jeannie, now, *they've* been here since they were born, they have. Friends too, since then.' He was silent for a minute or two, before adding, 'Used to be plenty of fishing hereabouts, quite a fleet put out from the loch, by all accounts. All gone now—'

They'd reached the end of the Old Village. They'd passed the boathouses where Iona kept the canoes and *Findhorn*.

No one there.

The road began to climb, swung inland. They took a track that curved into a wood, turned between large stone gates.

Avenues of gigantic beeches filtered the light and at the far end the house stood in silhouette against the loch. They drove into the yard between the vans and brick stacks. There was someone splashing water about with a hose.

'Kenny,' Ferry-Bob hailed him, getting out of the car and going over. 'Where's Annie?'

Kenny jerked his head towards the house. Ben remembered him from that first visit here, sitting in the kitchen. He was tall, very lanky, dark; he wore his hair in a long pony-tail and was a plasterer and joked a lot with Iona, who liked him. The tea-break was a celebration of his handiwork in the kitchen, and later they'd stopped to watch him sweep new expanses of pink on the ceiling in the passage.

He was scraping trowels and mixing boards under running water. He looked up at Ben's shadow. 'Iona's friend Ben it is, isn't it?'

Encouraged, Ben asked, 'Is she around?'

Kenny turned off the hose and thought about it. He shook water from the tools. 'Not been about much the past week . . .'

'She was teaching me to sail,' volunteered Ben. 'But then she didn't come yesterday, or today . . .'

'Ah,' said Kenny. He wiped the trowels with a rag, considering. 'She comes and she goes her own way, that girl. But I'll tell her you're looking . . .'

'Just that I was asking. I'm—'

Afraid, he thought, and stopped. *Can't say that.*

Kenny ignored the broken sentence. 'Aye, OK, I'll tell her. When I see her. I'll keep a look out . . .' He stacked the tools in buckets. 'Like the sailing, do you?' he wanted to know.

'Being out on the water. In the canoes too.' It was a relief to answer it – a kind of excuse for all the questions: just missing the boats, that's all . . .

'It's the way to get about here, it is,' agreed Kenny. He took up two of the buckets, indicated another, and went towards the house with a loping, long-legged stride. Ben picked up the load and followed. He put the bucket where Kenny showed him and waited, but already Kenny was caught in a shouted conversation up the stairs.

Ben wandered out again and round the side of the house.

There was new scaffolding here. This side of the house was thickly wooded, trees throwing deep shadow. Ferry-Bob was there with Annie. She was frowning, emphatic.

'I *thought* she was with Michael at the boat. I've no idea where she'll be if not there. It's hectic here, Ferry-Bob, *I* haven't seen her properly – just for a short while at bedtimes and breakfasts . . . She's always a one for coming in late, going out early . . . I thought—'

'Och, it's no matter. It's the lass's business, not ours,' Ferry-Bob stopped her. 'She'll be fine. Just off in her own world, no doubt. We were just wondering. We miss the lass, that's all – don't we, Ben lad?'

'Miserable this morning, she was,' Annie interrupted. 'She hasn't been sleeping well. But I'm *sure* she said she was coming to see you. I *should've* listened properly,' she fretted, pushing hair off her face, planting her hands on her hips, tilting her head and looking at Ben. 'Did you two quarrel maybe?'

'No!' Ben blurted, startled.

'Och, it's nothing like that, Annie, not the lad's fault,' said Ferry-Bob quickly, certainly. 'No, no, Annie . . .'

There was a shriek from the mobile phone. Annie grimaced and turned away, lifting it to her ear.

Somebody rattled down a ladder from the scaffolding, fetched something, rattled back up again. Ben watched him climb. The plastic sheeting was off and charred rooftimbers exposed.

Ferry-Bob followed his gaze. 'Bit of a fire that was, all right. Bit of a mystery too, by all accounts. Did you hear the story that the fellow disappeared the same night – seventy years back or thereabouts? Grandson of the laird of the time or something. He turned up in some foreign place, years later. Never came back, mind, died abroad – so I heard.'

Annie was tucking the phone back in her pocket. 'Ferry-Bob, this place'll be the death of me . . .' she shook her head and her face furrowed with a new frown. '. . . sure it's going to be, sure as anything! Now he's wanting to move the finish date forward! An opening party in a few weeks, would you believe!' She smiled wanly and went away towards the yard.

'Ah we-ell,' sighed Ferry-Bob. 'We'll go now, eh, Ben?' His hand on Ben's shoulder tried to encourage. Ben took a final glance round. They walked back to the car and got in.

Ferry-Bob started the engine. Gloom, Ben thought, was something you could almost see, sitting between them. He was beyond shaking it off.

The mood was split suddenly by Kenny's face at the driver's window. 'I've been thinking, Ferry-Bob,' big grin, loud voice, 'there's the old rowboat, that Ben here could be using if he's a fancy to be out on the water. Get about a bit under his own steam, that way. The boat's pulled up on the shore a way down—'

'Now *that's* what I call a fine offer,' approved Ferry-Bob enthusiastically. Relief made his face shine. 'You're a good lad, Kenny. Ben here's pining for the open sea!'

Startled, surprised, pitched out of his misery, Ben said, 'Thanks!' answering the broadness of Kenny's grin with one of his own.

'That's on your friend Iona's say-so,' Kenny said. 'You've a good touch for the boats, she told me. I just have a need to get out to my brother's boat when he's down for a bit of fishing, so the rowboat's sitting idle at the minute. You give him a hand with taking it to Michael's bit of shore, Ferry-Bob, it'll be OK to keep it there. Just be sure to pull it clear of the tides, Ben.' To Ferry-Bob he added, 'You'll find the oars at my house – take them when you fancy. And you tell that Michael there's a letter waiting for him at the ferry pub – Jamie there's got it propped on the shelf.'

Kenny winked, straightened, banged the car-roof in farewell. Ferry-Bob shifted gears and pulled away, saluting as they entered the avenue.

Ben waved too, his mood lighter, eager. 'Lending a boat to a stranger!' he exclaimed. He was thinking: if I can get out there I can find her. Maybe she won't mind me looking, maybe it's just that she's got something else on and all this (he couldn't think what to call it) is made up in my own stupid mind.

'You're no stranger,' Ferry-Bob retorted. 'Anyway, Kenny's family: he's my cousin Bob's nephew on his wife's side . . .'

Ben had lost track, laughing. And he was looking out for the stretch of shore beyond the village, scanning for the boat.

They found it half-hidden in reeds, turned upside down against the rain, its faded red paint merging with the shingles. Together they heaved it over, brushed blown leaves and cobwebs away. Each took an end and felt its weight.

'You'll manage that fine,' confirmed Ferry-Bob. 'We'll go now for the oars, and find this letter for Michael while we're about it.'

They stopped to tell Michael. He drove with them to the ferry pub, went in, came out, no letter in sight.

Later, at the cottage, he took it from his back pocket, still sealed, airmail blue and stuffed with something bulky. Ben saw him. He saw Michael throw it in a drawer, and push the drawer shut. He caught a glimpse of other envelopes inside.

Ferry-Bob saw it too, and caught Ben's eye. 'Another letter he won't read! Ben, Ben, y'r uncle's a strange man and that's a fact.'

And for a brief, tempting moment Ben was going to tell

him about the waking in the middle of the night to find the lights still on, Michael outside pacing the shore. Never asleep. Never calm.

But there was something too private in it; it was a betrayal to have seen it, to say it, even to Ferry-Bob, who was a friend. He didn't know really what he could say. And so – again – he said nothing.

Ten

He had rowed out on flat water beneath a dull sky. Now mist rolled in across the heights, and a rising wind whipped the waves to a vicious chop.

He wanted to cross the loch, heading for *Rudha Dhubh*. But the boat tossed and pitched, waves broke over the bows, water slopped in the bottom, and he saw he was fighting a current set to sweep him down the loch. The tide in full spate -- wind against tide, he thought, and was furious with himself. She would have known that, and he felt her absence more keenly. He'd not even had the sense to check for something to bale out the boat! Nothing in his brain but his drive to get out and look for her. Stupid!

He stopped rowing and searched for the baler. With relief he found it wedged below a thwart, and he spent some minutes scooping up water and throwing it overboard. All the time, though, the current was pushing him sideways, away from *Rudha Dhubh*, and so he started to row again.

Ten minutes on and he had made little headway from the shore. The oars were so different from canoe paddles, their weight and length more difficult to manage than he'd expected, the current too strong.

He abandoned the effort to cross. Instead he turned along the loch, travelling with the inward push of the water. Distances still deceived. Unexpected islands lifted from the water; the loch felt longer, broader with the heaving effort of the oars than ever it had seemed with the skimming speed of *Ulaidh* or *Findhorn*'s flight across its waters. He seemed to be working away for an age yet moving little, measured against the long, pale line of the shore.

He had been awed by the magnificence of the mountains around him. Now he saw only their inhospitable crags, the sheer fall to cold loch waters; lonely shores; barren rock-ridges.

Yet for all this, his mood had changed. He had woken with a hard, clenched-teeth determination. To break out of this pervading helplessness. The terror – he could only admit it was terror – fought with the belief that she *was* out there and he must find her.

Something's wrong.

For the moment it gave him a kind of energy: hopeful despite the dread that nudged relentlessly at the back of his mind.

He had slept badly. Dreams crowded closer. Michael had tried to be cheerful over breakfast, but the shadows of his own face confirmed what Ben already knew: lights flooding the cottage till nearly dawn, sleepless pacing . . .

He had said to Michael: 'You were up a lot last night.' He wanted to ask: *Why can't you sleep?*

But Michael's light, casual, 'I can't sleep when it's hot,'

stopped him. It was a dismissal. He'd finished breakfast, told Michael he was going out in Kenny's rowboat, shoved it down the beach and into the loch.

Look as hard as he might, though, there was no thread on the water that might be *Ulaidh* or *Tapuru*, no yellow triangle of *Findhorn*'s sail.

He came to shores where he'd swum or explored with Iona. He left the boat and climbed through heather-slopes to where they'd watched the eagles.

He felt only the silent weight of the glen beneath lowering mists. And there was a stench that turned his stomach. It rose all around him, along with a droning of flies in the heavy stillness. *Something rotten.*

He stumbled across it below the crag where they'd sat. The carcass sagged, half-hidden in the reeds of a bog. It lay on its back, the torso gaping red where something had torn it, its sad sheep's face gazing dully at flies swarming in the air above.

He gagged and turned away, not wanting to see. But in the next moment he was angry at this wrecking of his bright memory of the place, at the insects that buzzed him like angry wasps, at the other sheep grazing placidly on the slope nearby. Their indifference felt like a kind of corruption.

Betrayal.

He thought suddenly, *it's what I've been doing.*

He shouted it aloud, and the yell was a release in the stifling silence. The sheep skittered away. Then they stopped, put their heads down and resumed feeding.

I've been doing that. I'm just wallowing about – worrying, waiting . . . What for? Someone to say what to do? Michael to see there's something wrong, so I don't need to explain? Kenny's boat? Ferry-Bob? Why?

He got back to the shore quickly and rowed on. The winds were calming, the water flatter, and it was a little easier. By late afternoon he'd reached the cliff below Shallachain House. He was hungry and very tired. He'd brought nothing to eat, not thinking he'd be out this long, not planning for a fruitless day's searching that just went on and on to nowhere.

He tied the boat to a boulder on the narrow weed-strewn beach and clambered up the bordering rocks. He squatted down. He looked back at the way he'd come, at the distant curve in the loch that took it out of sight past Michael's place. He was dispirited by all this effort that had brought nothing, and his gaze drifted downwards, to the rocks drying below.

He'd not been back here since Iona first brought him to the house. But it came to him slowly, seeping upwards like the kind of awareness that comes as you rise from deep sleep to full waking: first sound; then colour and shape; then, bit by bit, a final, full, clear focus . . .

This was the place of his dream.

There was the angle of rock where waves snatched at the body of a girl.

With the knowledge came panic. He leapt to his feet. He felt pain in his hands. They were torn and blistered, they stung. Blood streaked his legs. He was drenched, waves welled around him, it was dark, wind battered him . . . And then the shock of recognition transformed to another kind of fear that stirred through him with a great wash of misery, longing, despair.

It was gone. Only a dull grey sky above a dull grey loch. No torn hands, no blood, no waves, no night – it was all in the night, he thought, and there was relief in realising it. *I'm never going to be here at night.*

He slid down the rocks to the beach and swiftly pushed the boat off, rowing as fast as he could, frantic to stop the images returning, driven by the notion that anywhere but here would be safe, pulling straight out towards the middle – anywhere to stop the pictures coming again.

Suddenly he was a long way out. The rocks and the little beach merged to a uniform dullness against the rise of the cliff. The houses of the Old Village were very distant. No sign of life.

And the wind had dropped. It was like a gasp, then the hush of a breath held. It spread from shore to shore like oil creaming the skin of the water.

Yet the boat was moving, swinging, swaying. He worked at the oars, trying to hold it steady, puzzled, uneasy. He looked around. Iona talked of the treachery of the loch: what next?

Movement nudged at the corner of his eye. Something black – flowing just beyond his vision. He turned his head towards it. He steadied his gaze.

Again. Closer. A flicker just above the water. Dark and glistening.

He thought, it's not above the water, it's coming from underneath.

A fluid coiling up, over, down.

Another. Up, over, down. And another – a rolling cycle of flowing loops that moved across the loch . . .

Then nothing.

He steered the boat round, scanning the waters.

Again. Closer still. This time he saw them clearly.

With a shock he understood they were circling him: four long, gleaming shapes, dark and smooth, flowing up from the water in a fluid spiral of leaps . . .

Porpoise? Dolphin? Fear gave way to awe – he couldn't take his eyes off them. It was all happening in silence: not even the swirl of water around them cast the slightest ripple of sound.

Up and over and down. Round and round and round.

Then nothing. He waited. He scoured the horizon and peered into the green depths beside the boat.

Gone.

But there was other movement. The water around him was gathering inwards, swelling. He had the extraordinary sensation it was lifting him and the boat underneath him. An odd, cold stillness rose with the smell of the sea, washed over him, fell back, died.

Again he was looking at ordinary water, under an ordinary overcast sky. Nothing menacing or unusual in it, just the threat of rain that had still not come.

Scared, he began to row. In vain he searched forward and back, side to side for the creatures that had ringed him.

He came in sight of Michael's beach. It was then he became aware of the heads of the seals behind. Following. Watching, he thought. Curious. Guarding. As if seeing me home.

Michael had been working on *Sea Hawk* all day. Over supper he said, 'I'll go down the coast – probably not tomorrow, maybe the next day. Soon, anyway. There's things I need to buy, and things I want to find out about: there's a wooden boatbuilder might be able to help. Fancy coming?'

'I'll probably stay here – if you don't mind,' said Ben.

'As you like.'

It was a new kind of silence between them. It was not so much in the lack of words as in the lack of meaning. They talked about the practical stuff – what to eat, where they were going. But facing him, Ben was tongue-tied about the strangeness on the rocks and the loch, for there were no words in his vocabulary to describe it. And Michael never sat still long enough for him to find a way to speak.

He did tell Michael about the leaping creatures. Porpoise – they must have been, Michael guessed. He'd spotted them travelling the loch earlier. Rare, in these waters, riding before a storm probably, he'd said, and gone off to look for a book to show Ben a picture.

He did ask if Ben had seen Iona. He said nothing when Ben answered no. Just got up from the table – and the meal, and the subject, had ended.

Ben put out from the shore again the next day. The clouds

had lifted a little. Here and there a pale sun broke through. Already the rowing was easier – not just because the waters stayed flat: it was more that his muscles were learning the stroke and pace of the oars.

'I'll go across the loch,' he'd told Michael. 'Just to the old lighthouse and back.'

For a fleeting moment Michael seemed about to say something. But he didn't. He did come down to the shore and help Ben push out the boat. Left on the beach his uncle seemed small, Ben thought. Lonely. He was taken by an impulse to return and try to cross the vacuum that was opening between them. Was it his fault, this – whatever it was – that had usurped their friendship? Was it his own weird moods?

Logically he knew it wasn't. What he hadn't said to Michael was matched by the things Michael hadn't said to him.

It ought to be so simple to ask him. About the letters for example . . . Why didn't Michael read them?

Not simple to get an answer.

Should I have an answer?

None of my business.

But he's *miserable*—

Already he could see Michael disappearing behind the cottage, going towards his van. Going to *Sea Hawk*. The thought of the boat brought the thought of Iona. The impulse to return warred with the impulse to look for her.

He put his back into the rowing and headed the boat straight out, across the narrowest part of the loch.

Eleven

He saw first the slender lines of *Tapuru* against the shore. He pulled the rowboat alongside and made his way across the rocks.

She stood on the other side of the old lighthouse, leaning against the wall.

'Iona.'

She whirled to face him: shadow-eyed, gaunt under the wild mop of her hair. She backed away, stopped, came towards him, stopped again.

Lamely he began, 'I came to the house. I wondered where you'd been – if you were all right.'

'I know – but I don't . . .'

He didn't prompt her. The words she might say threatened him, thin in the silence. *I don't want to see you.*

He saw the hollows of her face, the extraordinary blueness of her eyes. He couldn't read her expression – an unfamiliar blankness that held him off.

Then her face creased like a small child holding back tears; abruptly she was crying – great juddering sobs; he was appalled by their ugly desperation and force and it left nothing but the need to staunch them, stop them, wrap his arms round her, and in a rush he did so – holding her very tight and very still and for a long time.

The sobbing began to slow. She shifted and glanced up at him. She flushed. She pulled out of the circle of his arms, turning away.

He didn't follow her, confused. She jumped down the rocks to the water's edge and rinsed her face. He watched her climb back towards him.

Again she threw him a glance. It was brief and uncertain – a pale smile that flicked away as soon as it had shown. There was a hotness in her cheeks.

He said again, keeping hold of the simple things that he could, 'I wondered if you were all right. I went up to the house to find out.'

'I know,' she said. Her voice was thick and tearful. 'I wanted to come down and see you – but you were at the boat, and I don't . . .'

She left it incomplete. She went to sit against the lighthouse wall and looked up at him. The smile flickered again.

He took it as a signal and sat down beside her.

'I'm so tired, Ben,' she said. '. . . can't sleep. Every night . . . night after night—'

She did not finish, and he did not have to ask. It seemed to him then as if everything – from the very beginning – had been working towards this moment. Since the day he'd

crossed on the ferry, since he'd first seen her beside *Sea Hawk*.
Through all the days he'd spent with her. Through all these
last miserable hours of wondering and searching.

In some small, still centre of himself he knew he had never
wanted anything so much in his life as he wanted this single
moment to last, to stay here with her and be able to stop her
misery. He did not care any more that he might give away
how much she mattered to him. He did not care about the
risk that he might not matter to her. He did not mind that he
might offer help and she might throw it back. It was simply
that his whole existence was rooted in the one task – to shield
her from whatever was gathering about them.

And it was gathering. He could feel it. It was not here,
with them now. But it was waiting.

And it was also *in* him – something he knew, or
remembered, or foresaw.

Sea Hawk. The anger. The dreams.

They're not dreams, he saw suddenly.

They're memories.

They had sat for some time without talking. Weak sunlight
had filtered through the cloud and touched the battered walls
of the old lighthouse. They leaned back, feeling its warmth
against their backs, hearing the screech of the gulls coming
and going in the upper chamber. In the frail sunshine, the
rocky shoreline was suddenly alive with swooping birds, the
nearer waters broken by the glossy heads of circling seals.

Iona seemed calmer. Yet now Ben found himself

unwilling to intrude on the silence. Her nearness was like a burn along the side of his body. Yet he was afraid that if he spoke she might retreat again.

She said suddenly, 'I'm just so tired. I'm scared of sleeping, Ben. Sort of pictures whenever I try to . . . like I'm watching from somewhere else, I'm looking at myself *in* them – d'you know what I mean? Sometimes they're two different pictures, sometimes they're muddled up together . . .'

Again he stayed quiet, and after a while she began again, 'There's one that keeps coming back. I'm looking at the house – it's bright, all lit up, but it's night, dark all around, though the house is brilliant. I'm on the lawn in front. There's someone else there too – don't know who, sometimes I think it's you, sometimes I can't see. Lights all over – streaming from the windows; music, people all over, walking about . . . At first, you see, I just thought it was a muddle in my head, imaginings mixed up with stories I heard from the owner – Annie's boss. He took us to dinner once and told us all about the house, and the fire that burned it down. So I thought it was just me imagining the grand parties there used to be there . . .' She paused, and then, speaking very quickly, as if wrestling with the story, dredging it all up from somewhere very deep, she said, 'One night, I even woke up *standing* on the lawn. I mean *really* there – in the middle of the night. I don't remember getting there, I don't remember unlocking the door – I was just there. I was so scared, Ben. I woke Annie and then she got worried and talked to the doctor . . .'

Noisily, she blew her nose, and when she had finished she leaned against him, closing her eyes. He put his arm round her. Then she was silent, sitting very still. He began to wonder if she'd fallen asleep.

But in a great rush she launched off again. As if she'd won a new struggle to make it clear and simple for him, for herself.

'But then there was this other dream too. It's always dark, and I'm so scared – there's someone shouting at me, sometimes I think they're crying or wailing . . . When I look at the house there are flames sparking up into the sky – a great bonfire way up. At first I kept telling myself I was just imagining the fire that burned the house down. But each picture kept coming back, you see, always just the same, and . . .' she paused and leaned away from him so that she could look into his face. '. . . you're going to think I'm crazy.'

He tightened his grip on her. He shook his head. He did not trust himself to say anything. Images whirled in his mind. Flames, the stench of scorching; a voice that resonated in him as if it flowed through his bones.

Iona had moved nearer. She seemed to be taking courage from his closeness. Her voice was losing its tearfulness, quieter, even matter-of-fact. 'I didn't hear it at first, you know – just felt strange at the boat. Like I wanted to stay for a long time. Not scary or anything. The way sometimes a place makes you peaceful – you know?'

He thought of that first time he'd seen her by the boat. How he'd wanted to stay, watching them both, in the bay.

'Then it changed. I can't remember when. I heard—'

73

The voice of my dreams, he thought. She heard the voice of *my* dreams. She is dreaming my dreams. I am dreaming her dreams.

The strangeness of it astonished him.

'I couldn't hear the words,' she was saying, 'but I could tell the anger. Then even you – and Michael – seemed to get angry with me. Horrible times when you were both cross. I just didn't want to stay.' She laughed nervously, 'So I went away. Then I wanted to tell you, but it all sounded impossible – no one would believe. I couldn't explain and you wouldn't know what I was on about. Then I couldn't come back because when I got near the bay I felt . . . odd. As if something was going to happen to me. Something really scary, Ben. Even at Michael's place. I got so scared.'

She looked about her, up at the lighthouse, at the wheeling gulls. 'This is the only place it isn't like that. Here it's always calm.'

Again Ben couldn't answer. He'd been thinking of the fire in his dream. He'd started to say, *I've seen something like that too*, but then the image of the girl in the water filled his head, and he couldn't tell her that.

'We'll work it out,' he muttered instead. 'It's the boat, Iona. There's something—'

He got no further. She had leapt to her feet. 'It's going to storm – we should have been watching.' She was staring to the west. A purpling bruise was spreading across the reddening rim of the sky, deepening, darkening, clouds building with heavy, rolling menace. It was getting late and the wind was rising. 'We should have been watching,' she said again. 'We need to go across quickly or we'll be stuck here. We should have moved before.'

He heard the urgency in her voice and followed her at a run down the rocks. They tied *Tapuru* to the rowboat and took an oar each. They pushed off and leapt in, sitting side by side on the thwart. They began to pull across the loch.

They were nearing the centre. He said to her, 'It's gone all calm.' It was like yesterday – the wind holding its breath, glassy smooth on every side, sound muted. He half expected to see the glint of a porpoise.

Towards the mouth of the loch there was a shadow. As if a line were drawn from shore to shore. Water gleamed before it, angry red in the flush of the lowering sun.

The line was moving towards them.

'Iona, what's that?'

She twisted round to look. Then she swung back at once and resumed rowing. 'A wave. Behind it'll be the wind and the rain. Row, Ben, row. *Don't* stop now!' Her voice was shrill with apprehension. 'We've got to get back quick – the boat's too small for a big storm. It'll just swamp us!'

He kept his eye on the advancing line. Already it was near enough for him to see that behind it the loch waters rippled and rolled. White horses capped the gathering breakers. They were still ahead of it, but only just.

The first spattering of rain caught them. They were close enough to the shore to see Michael waiting. By the time they reached the beach a gusting squall slapped them and threw the boat at the beach. They leapt out, struggling to pull it out of the water, its bulk bucking and rocking in the chop, the canoe surging wildly in its wake. Ben waded in to catch it and was bowled over. He floundered, lost his balance, toppling helplessly into icy surf. Water gushed into his mouth and nose and he scrambled to his feet, choking.

Michael hauled him clear of the next breaker. 'Inside, both of you. Ben, strip off and get straight into the shower to warm up. Iona, I'll drop you home in the van. Just dry off a bit first.'

She stopped him as they ran for the cottage. 'I'm OK Michael – really. If you'd just take me home, please, Annie'll be so worried – she won't know I'm safely here.'

Gone. Before he could speak to her again. No more than a brief backward glance and a small, warm smile at him as she climbed into the van.

Afterwards, though, it was the glance that Ben could hold on to. It was solid and real and alive. It was something that told him she would return.

Twelve

The cottage was empty. He could tell as he woke. There was a silence sharpened by the rattle of rain against the window and an unfamiliar rippling twilight in the room.

He stumbled into the sitting room, hoping he was wrong and that Michael was there.

Only the room in deep shadow.

He went to the window to look down at the loch. Rain swept in driving sheets across the water. Hills and shores were blotted out. Even the headland had disappeared in the mists.

There was a note on the table.

Ben,

Got off pretty early as hoped. Filthy day – <u>don't</u> go out on the water – PROMISE. Gales forecast. Nearly woke you to check if you wanted to come with us – but you looked beat, so sleep's probably best. Sorry to leave you with a dull day ahead. Annie's fairly desperate for a co-driver (car's been playing up and they can't spare anyone at the house with the ludicrous deadline on finishing the work). I was going to do the drive down the coast anyway – so it's

the least I can do. Should be back on the last ferry. Hope you find
enough to do for the day — check out books and magazines in my
room. I think there's some about these lochs somewhere. Top of the
bookcase?

Maybe get more sleep — you really looked worn out last night. See
you. M

He stood in sleep-fuzzed confusion. He remembered
Michael's return last night. He'd been asleep in the chair,
swamped by the day's events and endless broken nights. He
dug out a vaguer memory of Michael ushering him to bed
with a drink and a sandwich. But he couldn't remember
anything said – not about Michael going with Annie today, at
least.

What now? He went back into the bedroom. Half a
sandwich and a mug of cold cocoa were still on the floor. He
fought the longing to crawl back into bed.

He sat on the edge. Sleep would be so much easier than
waking, facing it all.

Yesterday, in the storm, left with just Iona's parting smile,
he'd made up his mind to talk to Michael straight away, as
soon as he was back from driving her home. About the
dreams – memories – whatever.

What were they? Hers. His. This restless nervousness – fear
– it was fear – it weaved its way into everything he did.

Makes no sense. Muddle after muddle.

Afraid of what?

Scared, she'd said she was.

Gathering – it was gathering. A mustering of shadows about him, a tremulous nudging loneliness as soon as the van had disappeared, and she with it, and Michael too.

In an effort to shed it, he'd gone to shower and put on dry clothes – ready to think it through: there must be *some* way to explain it, something they could *do*.

Talk to Michael and Ferry-Bob – Ferry-Bob would listen.

But now, today – failure. No chance with Michael last night. None this morning. And the tangled hours of the night were returning: in and out of drifting half-sleep, sudden wakings, exhausted plunges into jumbled visions of water, fire, the shadows of Shallachain House, the beam of a lighthouse, Iona. And somewhere a ceaseless, harrowing screaming . . .

He could remember one picture that was different: a sunny day, a paddle steamer bedecked with flags, crowded with people. A happy dream: it *was* a dream, he thought, a real one, not a memory become nightmare, and for a while after he'd woken from it he'd dwelled on it, its lightness something to ward off other images shaping in the dark.

Why a steamer? He'd never been on one. He *had* leafed through a book – there was one somewhere about boats that once travelled the lochs.

Dig it out again. Something concrete he could do—

What would Iona be doing? He wanted to speak to her, but the phoneless cottage thwarted him.

Must move. *Do* something.

He showered and dressed, ducking through the rain to the

outhouse bathroom and returning thankfully to dry warmth and the prospect of breakfast. He was ravenous. He shoved bacon and tomatoes under the grill, and the activity lifted his spirits. He took his mug of tea to the window while everything cooked. It was getting darker. Wind-driven rain whirled in white flurries across the shore and now even the loch was obscured by billowing curtains of mist.

He switched on a few lights, and the room felt better. Safer.

I should have told her properly that she's not going mad. *We're in this together. Somehow. We'll work it out.* He wanted to yell that across the miles that separated them.

It had seemed so clear as he watched her leave yesterday. He'd stood in the shelter of the kitchen doorway as the wheels spun on the mud and the van lurched forward through the dripping trees. Just talk to Michael and Ferry-Bob – *tell them* . . . anything, something, maybe some of it would become clearer for the telling.

Now—

But one more day can't matter. We've talked, she'll feel better, not so alone, less scared.

I'm less scared, he told himself.

He wasn't. The day menaced him; exhaustion nudged, and he was again afraid to sit down for too long in case he fell asleep. He'd long forgotten the peace of dream-free sleep, dream-free waking.

He ate the bacon and tomato wedged between slices of toast, sitting at the table with a pile of magazines. Glossy lifestyle stuff; a travel magazine; comics – mostly last year's issues. Like a doctor's waiting room, he thought – probably left by people who'd stayed here on holiday. A few tourist brochures and a list of useful phone numbers. Local newsletters: arguments about land for a new playground; arguments about replacing the ferry with a bridge. Marauding stags eating crops. Reviews: church-hall concerts; summer fairs; agricultural shows, sheep-shearing contests. Reminiscences of the one-time fishing fleets hereabouts . . .

He wasn't in the mood. He finished eating, dumped the plate and mug in the kitchen and wondered what to do next. He switched on more lights and with an effort at finding something to keep him from thinking, decided to go in search of the book on steamers.

He found it on the shelf in Michael's room. He sat down again at the table, trying to make himself feel purposeful. He opened the book and turned the pages. There were pictures of steamers crossing the lochs below plumes of smoke; of passengers waiting at little stone jetties as steamers docked. Cars and sheep balanced precariously on small ferrying rowboats. A lorry dangled in a sling above a deck. One was taken from below, looking up at people leaning from the deck and pointing to the bulge of the broad, curved paddle box on the steamer's side.

Then it hit him, with the punch of a physical shock.

Kelda. He saw that dream again. On a jetty she stood waving – and he was standing *at the rail of a steamer*. Just like this one in the picture. He was leaning over to watch the paddles churn. He could see the creamy froth of water cascading off them. He looked up and saw Kelda. Her face was flushed pink from running – not an old woman's face, not the Kelda of now, but the face of a girl he *knew* was Kelda, and beside her stood someone else – someone whose gleeful jump and shout to catch his attention filled him with lightness.

Margaret, he said aloud. Margaret: the name rich with flocking memories.

I don't know anyone called Margaret, Ben thought in panic.

Stricken, he stood up and his chair fell with a bang – with a bang the memory swamping him. The face of Margaret was the face of Annie, Iona's mother, and he was crying now, but not him crying, he was filled with a kind of terror for himself, for Iona, for their separation, for his distance from her. He snatched open the door to run into the storm to the house on the cliff where she was.

Rain burst through the doorway, a puddle forming and flooding across the uneven floor as lightning flared and a blast of wind flung the door back against the wall.

He grabbed it and pushed it shut again.

Got to stop this. Got to move. Be busy.

She'll be fine. She's at the house. Not alone – Kenny and the others there. Michael and Annie'll be back in no time . . .

He went into the kitchen. There were the plates Michael had left earlier, mugs . . . He ran hot water into the bowl, squirted in soap, loaded his own plate and mug, collected up Michael's . . .

Later, his eye fell on the little desk. On top lay the fragment of name-plank from *Sea Hawk*, where he'd put it. Below, the drawer was half open. The desk lamp lit up the edge of envelopes.

Michael's letters. It seemed to him, standing looking at them, that Michael's secret misery was all of a piece with his own, with the misery that welled from *Sea Hawk*. It was a new thought and it drove him suddenly across the room to pull the drawer wide open.

He counted the envelopes. Eight of them: all airmail. He picked up one. Canadian stamp. He put it down again.

Dishonest, prying – dishonest not asking and then trying to find out, dishonest not *talking* to him. He wished Michael would come back, then he could ask, insist on answers – some of this confusion might stop then.

He stared down at the letters again. On an impulse he picked up another and looked at the stamp. It was dated early June, and he calculated: nine weeks ago. He scanned the others. Some went back to April – that was about the time Michael'd come back from Canada. None opened.

Wrong. There was one. He could see a slit envelope, slightly torn, the letter poking out.

He shifted the other envelopes aside to uncover it properly. It lay half across some photographs. A group of kids, arms round each other's shoulders. Six of them – four girls and a couple of boys. They were in front of a row of sailing dinghies and behind them was what seemed to be a boathouse.

The next photo showed the same kids posing and laughing in the boats. He took another look at the envelope. Different handwriting. The other letters all had the same writing, every one of them. This was different, definitely.

At the bottom of the drawer lay a sheet of paper and he pulled it out. Application form for a job: '*boating and swimming instructor*' in Michael's writing. He'd filled in his name and the date – 3 May – but nothing else.

Suddenly Ben slid it back under the envelopes and shut the drawer. He thought: it's like reading someone's diaries – snooping. I shouldn't look. Then he thought, I *should*. If he won't tell me anything, how can I help?

He was startled by a flicker of lightning that lit every corner of the room. He waited for the crack of thunder. It came with a low, rumbling menace. He went to the window to look out.

Would Michael tell Annie anything? It was depressing that he might, but not ever tell Ben.

He thinks I'm too young. Maybe I am. Maybe this is all too much for me. Maybe he'll tell Annie, and get it off his chest, and he'll come back OK and he'll be able to listen, to see what's happening, make sense of it, and all this will be over – whatever it is.

But the thought of Annie brought the face of Margaret who had sprung from his dream and an anger throbbed through him with the drum of a voice – it was his own voice, yet it came from outside too, from the walls of the cottage, from the green flare of lightning across the loch and the crack of thunder very, very close.

STOLEN . . . MY LIFE . . . MINE
STOLEN

The lights quivered, went out, fluttered on again, held for a moment, and then died.

Thirteen

He woke with a start, and he was in the chair, stiff and cold. Pitch black in the cottage. By the luminous dial on his watch he could see the time: half past eleven. The electricity had been down since just after three.

Michael not back yet.

He pushed himself out of the chair, wincing at the cramp in his legs. He fumbled for the torch he'd put on the table.

'They're driving round the head of the loch,' Ferry-Bob had dropped by to tell him, earlier. Michael and Annie had phoned him at home. 'They can't get to the last ferry – the direct way's cut off – heavy flooding and there's been a fair mud slide further down. So they're taking the long way round. Anyway, the ferry's not running – seas too heavy.'

He'd delivered this spurt of news as he peeled the hood of his sodden coat back and stamped his boots on the mat. 'Fancy coming back to my house for a bite to eat?' he'd pressed on. 'Plenty for another mouth. Wait there for Michael to get back?'

Ben wanted to plead *take me to Iona*. Instead he'd managed

a lame, 'Thanks, I'll be OK here.' And then, in a burst of determination: 'Where's Iona?'

'She'll be fine, Ben. There's Kenny and the other lads staying over to watch the place. And her Auntie too – for a few days. The lass has company.'

'Ferry-Bob—' Ben had steeled himself to begin. But the wind surged furiously round the cottage, blasted rain at them, banged a shutter, and Ferry-Bob hadn't heard, hurriedly flipping up his hood and hunching away towards the car. 'We-ell, if you're sure—' the gale whipped his next words away.

'I'll be OK,' Ben had yelled.

I will be, he'd told himself. She will be.

But now, alone in the darkness, the silence stretched beyond the cottage. He could hear no wind. He opened the door to the loch and switched on the torch. A steady hissing rain was falling and the torchbeam carved a white path through it.

Why was Michael not back yet? Unease sent a shiver that was not cold but a nagging foreboding. He shut the door again and went into the kitchen and tried to think about getting something to eat. At least he'd feel warmer.

He stood irresolute.

And then it came, forcing itself forward in his mind, seeping through all his senses, though he'd been fighting it since he woke. Tonight there'd been something different in the restless sleep. Not like a dream. He'd been awake, actually there, *seeing it*, hearing, smelling, touching.

The lawns of Shallachain House. And the figure of a girl.

He'd been standing beside her. He'd felt rain on his skin. He'd watched the girl move. She'd walked steadily, slow but not hesitant. At first she'd seemed to be heading for the path through the bracken to the cliff. But he'd watched her turn aside and take the branching track along the cliff that wound in shallow, sloping descent through copses of trees, across a stile on the outer wall of the estate, and down to the Old Village and the long shore below.

This was not like the other pictures of his dreams – always fragmented, confused, twisted up with each other in a way that exhausted him, impossible to unpick from the muddle. That was another reason he couldn't explain it to anyone else.

Tonight's picture was sharp, stark. He could even see the girl's figure now, as he stood fully awake in the darkened kitchen of Michael's cottage with a torch in his hand. She was outdoors. She was in the rain in the middle of the night. She was walking down the path to the village and the shore.

It was happening now. *Now.* She was heading for the shore. She was heading for the boathouse where *Findhorn* and the canoes were kept.

The girl was Iona.

The certainty paralysed him.

Then the paralysis broke – there was no one to stop her, no one *knowing* she was alone, sleepwalking towards the water. No one knowing she was going to the canoes, to the vast deepness of the loch. He fled to the door and pulled it open and instinctively switched off the torch.

The loch stretched black in front of him, like a great dark cave hung with a canopy of mists and the echoing hiss of the rain. He flung the door closed, and went rapidly into his room, pulling open the cupboard where his rain gear hung, still unused.

Now that he'd decided, he was calmer. The certainty gave a direction. He wanted to be organised, sensible, prepared. He tugged the coat on, and went into Michael's room to look for another torch. He couldn't find one. He searched the kitchen and found one in a bottom drawer among candles and spare batteries.

He shoved what he could into his pockets and went back to the door. He switched the torch off again. Let your eyes adjust, Michael always told him. Torchlight narrows your vision, blinds you to everything but the beam.

After a moment he pulled up his hood, closed the door behind him and stepped into the rain. He was banking on the rowboat still being where they'd hauled it the day before. He set off towards the invisible shore.

The canoe was still tied on. He heaved it higher, well clear of any tides. He undid the linking rope and shunted the rowboat down the shingles.

He pushed off into the water and leapt in.

Fourteen

Where was he going? He had a picture in his mind, that was all, and it drew him on across the hidden face of the loch. He seemed to travel in a tunnel, dark and echoing, loud with the beat of the rain on his hood and its deeper drumming on thwarts and boards and gunwales of the boat.

The oars were slippery with wetness. His hands numbed. Knuckles clenched white round the oar-shafts. He'd forgotten gloves, boots, waterproof trousers. His tracksuit bottoms dripped, feet squelched in slopping trainers. There was only the steady pull at the oars to keep him warm – a mesmeric rhythm that took all his strength: lean forward, heave back, forward, back . . .

He could see nothing but the pale wake of the boat unroll across the swirl of the current, and he watched its direction anxiously. Was he pulling evenly on the oars, moving in a straight line into the darkness that crowded at his back?

He twisted round and searched the direction he was rowing. On all sides the shore hid behind the hissing mask of the rain. Once, he caught a feeble light from high up. He thought it might be Shallachain House on the cliff, and then he thought it wasn't – there was nothing to help him, no point of reference to show it was far or near, high or low, moving or standing still . . .

Car lights swept out of the gloom and beamed over the water. Instinctively he snatched up the torch and flashed it towards them. What was Morse Code for 'help'? Three short, three long, three short – or the other way round? At the beginning (only days ago?) Iona had taught him . . .

The torchbeam died in the rain mist beyond the boat. No one would see it from shore. The car lights bobbed on, swung in an arc, disappeared.

He set himself square with the oars again. He rowed on towards the cliff.

Don't go out on the water, Michael had said.

Why did you go out on the water? Michael would ask later.

What was the answer?

In his mind Ben saw the girl of his nightmares. She rolled in the waves; her dead face looked at him.

Was it happening now, tonight? Would it be Iona's face, but he hadn't realised that before?

From his exhausted brain he dragged the vision again – the battering pulse of the storm; himself – torn and bloodied on the rocks. And suddenly there was hope in seeing it, for it was different from the new picture he'd seen tonight. Tonight's image was clear, sharp, unequivocal – as clear as if he moved beside Iona – walking on the path to the boats.

Iona *alive*.

It had not happened yet. There was time.

But not time to run along the shore over rocks and bogs and beaches – miles of it, just to reach the village for help. Later, when he came to explain, he would say that to Michael – *only the boat could get me there fast*.

It was the loch that called her. The loch – and the cliff and rocks below the house. He knew it with a peculiar, bleak certainty. And what frightened him more was no longer just a belief it would happen. As he moved into the darkness of the loch it seemed to him that part of him was summoning her, drawing her towards it, *making it happen*.

He faltered. This was beyond his strength, this journey across the water, its unseen possibilities.

He blinked his eyes clear of the drizzle, clear of the exhaustion. He set the oar-shafts firm in the rowlocks. He steadied his grip, sat square on the thwarts. Again he began the steady, rhythmic pull – watching the oars dip and lift, taking him closer and closer to the place where she would go, where he must find her, must stop it happening.

He came beyond the bend of the loch. He knew this because he could see frail lights from the Old Village and for a moment the headlamps of another car that travelled for a short distance, stroked the white square of a building, stopped and switched off.

Row in and get help? He remembered thinking that, like a question phrased by another – someone quite outside himself, someone calm and logical and nothing to do with the stark conviction that drove him. He answered without stopping, heaving and breathing and heaving again against the cramp in his muscles and his fingers frozen to claws round the oars.

In the time needed to reach the Old Village, he could also reach the cliff.

By the time a search party could leave, it would be over.

The rain stops. It is quite sudden, and it leaves behind a peculiar hushed silence, broken only by the splash of his oars.

And then gurglings – whispers of bubbling sound so faint he almost misses them.

Nervously he thinks of the porpoise. He wonders, looks around. He sees that the circle of the oars' movement is aglow. Light sparks from the dripping wood. It's like shards of ice: arcs of glitter – silver, green, blue – the burn of an ice-fire cold in the darkness, and the wake across the water fizzes too – purple-green, blue, silver, a river of sparkling fire – he can almost hear the crackle.

Puzzlement becomes fear. Then with sudden relief he recognises it: *plankton in the water* – Iona told him about it (they make their own light, we'll go out one night so you can see, she'd promised). Calmer with the knowledge, the weird beauty of it catches him. Curious, he thinks he *will* ask her, later . . .

Ripples and eddies loop in silver circles round him. Then it is more than the movement of the oars – it is a restless bubbling from somewhere below, a turbulence heaving and swelling and seething upwards and the boat rocks with the thrust – bow to stern, side to side – it flings him about, he grabs at the gunwale, loses the oars, lunges for them, grips the shafts fiercely, rows faster, straining to cross the turmoil, his muscles shrieking with effort, his breath coming in short, hard gasps. *Get out of reach, away . . .*

A savage convulsion shoots him forwards. And where the boat passes he sees a shape gather, drawing the current inwards, upwards, darkening and thickening. Then it erupts, glittering water pours from it – he is petrified – some giant creature of the loch is rising and he rows frantically away as the shape lifts, takes form – the hull of a boat, its great curving nose that soars vertically and then subsides sideways, slowly, to lie across the surface of the water.

Darkness closes in. The shape recedes into the rain that has begun to fall again, relentless, veiling all.

Has he seen it? Is it another memory – or a figment of his imagination? *A premonition?*

He swings to look behind him. Is that the cliff? He isn't sure. He hopes, pleads, scans for it again.

He turns back to the oars, resumes rowing.

A new shape looms. It rises above the line of shore that he has just found in the darkness. His heart pounds at what he might see.

It's not Iona.

A canoe, impaled on a rock. Empty – he can just see that,

coming close in to it. It leans, part-submerged, the torn edge of its gash half out of the water.

Ulaidh.

He casts wildly around for Iona. But the darkness is a solid wall blocking the frailty of the torchbeam. He sees a gap in the rocks. He puts the boat between the ridges and surges forward to a beach. The tide is already up and the weed-strewn shingles are covered. In the gloom it is unfamiliar, bordering rocks throwing unknown shadows against him, peaks and hollows difficult to decipher, distances baffling.

He leaves the boat and clambers upwards. He is trying to find the place where he sat so few days ago, where he recognised the rocks of the dream.

Is it here? He isn't sure. Then he is, and swings the torch left and right, up and down.

Empty. Rock-slabs glisten and the seaweed rustles with pattering rain. Something scuttles from the probing beam of the torch.

Panic is overtaking. He tries to push it back, think clearly. He moves further on. Stay calm, walk carefully. He mustn't trip or slide and fall – it'd ruin everything, both of them on the rocks needing help, unable to help her.

She lies below, face down.

It is a steep cleft, filling fast with the tide, and it is not a place he's been before, not the place of his dream. The difference brings a surge of hope: it won't be the dead, blank face that stares at him from the pool.

Waves are already nudging, seeking to lift her.

He slithers down and nearly falls. He recovers his footing and straddles the crevice. He braces his feet across the gap so that he can bend to her without falling. Water bursts through a hollow below with a deep boom, gushes up. It seeps into the cleft where she lies and froths across her outstretched arm.

She is limp, blank, flopping when he tries to lift her. In the darkness her flesh is blue. He holds his hand to her nose and mouth. Faint warmth, breath on his palm. He takes off his coat and wraps it round her, gets his arms underneath her and tugs her higher, hastily trying to judge how high the tide will come, how to get her to somewhere safe, flat, out of reach.

She is heavy. He has to prop her weight while he searches for his next foothold. He has to stop again and again on the jagged, slippery rock – to catch his breath, to adjust his hold, to brush rain and sweat from his eyes.

At the top of a long slab there is a flat area, high, drier, tucked in below the overhang of the cliff.

Leave her here. Fetch help.

He calculates: the village is an hour's row away, even going straight across the end of the loch to it. Shallachain House is just above him: up the path on the cliff.

He looks up. Where? From here he can't see the path. He remembers its steepness, their breathless climb on that hot afternoon.

The rain is heavier, a drenching beat on his shirt.

She'd said, 'Not in the wet – you slide straight off.'

Her stillness, her coldness, terrifies him.

He looks again at the cliff.

After, he has no real memory of it. Fragments remain. Mud
– an oozing, treacherous slime. Hands raw, grabbing
handholds on tree roots, heather, corners of rock. A helpless
slide to a ravine becomes a torrent of rainwater and broken
branches. A bone-jarring thud as he lands against a boulder,
the torch bouncing from his hand, clatters against rock, light
arcing in slow cart-wheels downwards into blackness.
Darkness up and down now, inching forward on hands and
knees to feel for the flatness of the path, its invisible twists and
bends through the boulders, the inward angles that will take
him upwards to safety and rescue, not down to the rocks and
the black loch waters.

Somewhere, sudden voices. A burst of light.

Noises – voices – loud, shrill. His name. Iona's. Shouting.

Hands and faces above him. The roar of a motor. Beams
strafing the loch from somewhere very high. Continuous
murmurs of sound – and voices, deep and quick and urgent,
and rushing movement – lights, wind, swirling wind, cold . . .

Cold. Very cold.

The scratch of a blanket.

Her name. *Iona*. His voice.

The motion of walking in a kind of numbness. A hand on
his arm. Hands on both arms, face, eyes, neck. Lights and
voices and faces in a sea of brightness, endless, opening . . .

Into the roar, climbing upwards.

PART THREE

SEA MOON

Fifteen

Bright yellow – it swirled and swung before his eyes and he fought to steady it, till the yellow gleamed brighter, stopped moving, came suddenly into focus.

He was lying on his back, gazing to his left. He moved his head and looked the other way. Bright yellow again. A curtain. He was lying on a bed enclosed by curtains.

There was a gap by his feet, and through it he could see someone in another bed. Footsteps, water running, a shrill phone, clank of something metal . . .

Voices – one was Michael's. Ben raised himself on one elbow and called.

Michael came through the break in the curtain. 'Ben,' he murmured, and to someone out of sight, 'He's awake.'

A woman appeared: nurse's uniform. 'Good. Sleep'll have done what's needed.' She wielded a large, encouraging grin. 'Quite a night you had . . .' Swiftly she came forward and reached for a holder on the wall beside the bed. She unclipped a thermometer, shook it, poked it into his mouth, pushed him gently back on the pillows, lifted his wrist, fingered his pulse, shook her head when he tried to speak.

Michael watched her. He was hunched and anxious, and with a glance she took a measure of him. 'You two can talk in a minute. Ben can probably go home after the doctor's been. And *you* should get some sleep,' she admonished. She left the thermometer in Ben's mouth and walked round the bed, pushing the curtains back against the wall. It revealed a large room lined with beds and expectant faces turned towards him. There was a wash-basin, someone running water into a flower vase, high windows and wan grey light from a drizzling sky. Somewhere a television murmured.

In a flash he remembered where he'd come from, what he'd seen – the beach and the storm, the cliff. He remembered voices, lights—

Iona.

He jerked upright and his head swam with the sudden movement. He flung his hand out to steady himself. The nurse frowned and took the thermometer from his mouth. 'Slowly does it, give yourself a chance . . .'

He appealed to her, to Michael, 'Where's Iona?'

Michael flicked a look at the nurse. Now she was busy yanking up the head of his bed and piling pillows against it. Her tone stayed energetically bright. 'Your friend's here, don't you worry your young head about that. She's in *very* good hands.' She swung a wheeled table across the foot of the bed, pushing it into place with her foot. 'Now, *your* task is warmth and food and good sleep in your own bed, and you'll be right as rain. I'll be off to get something for you to eat.

Then your orders are: bath, dress, and we'll have you on your way.' She smiled at him to belie the no-nonsense tone, strolled away, swung round to wag a finger for emphasis. 'That's *after* the doctor, mind.' She pushed her way out of the ward through swing doors.

In the lull of her absence Michael stayed silent. He was trying to organise his words, and Ben saw that and a coldness seized the pit of his stomach.

Into the lengthening silence, he insisted, '*Michael, where—*?'

'Here,' his uncle interrupted. 'Like the nurse said, Ben, Iona's here, in good hands. But—' He shrugged. It was a hopeless, despairing kind of movement. 'She hasn't come round, Ben. They don't know why – no concussion or broken bones, no sign of a fall, and she hasn't been deep in the water – not drowned, I mean. But she's unconscious. We'll have to wait—'

He broke off. Again he hunched his shoulders, pushed his hands in his pockets. Then he took them out again as if not knowing what to do next. He repeated, agitated, 'She hasn't drowned. She's in a sort of coma, but she hasn't *drowned*.'

Ben subsided against the pillows. All this, and nothing . . .

'Annie's with her. They kept you in for observation – you were so cold – exposure, wet through . . .' Michael's voice trailed off.

Ben had looked away. He'd said nothing.

Nothing to say.

Failure. All he'd tried to do, and yet failure.

'I want to see her,' he muttered.

She lay small and narrow beneath the blankets. Machines ringed her – tubes, lights, dials. Annie sat in a chair, elbows resting on the bed, one hand propping her head, the other spread on the fingers of Iona's hand. Her face was greyed and thinned by fatigue, hair awry, eyes closed, though she was upright on the edge of the chair, as if poised for the slightest motion from the inert shape in the bed.

Michael leaned over and whispered. '*Annie.*' She stirred, woke with a start, leapt to her feet in confusion.

'Michael – Ben, you're all right! Oh, that's very good, that's good.'

Michael said, 'I'll take him home, Annie, but I'll be back as soon as I can – give you a break, and then—'

'I don't want to go,' Ben said. There was a murmuring in his head. It came in the moment that Annie spoke – an imperceptible echo, like a distant calling from a long way off. But it was growing, even as he saw them turn to look at him, even as he gazed into Annie's tired face. And the echo was becoming words, though they were not words he could hear, and with the words came anger, seeping through every bone and sinew of his body, strengthening, spreading, mounting till it was a pulse like a heartbeat from inside him, from the machines that held Iona and the walls and beds and cupboards of the ward. It was anger, yet it was grief too, and loneliness, and the anger was at Iona and himself, and everyone else in the room and beyond – in the houses of the village and the people of the loch, the ones he knew and the ones he did not know. He saw himself alone, abandoned; he wept for his loss, for the loss of others, his pain was a storm wave gathering to surge and smash across the rocks, and above the storm there was a long, trailing wail like the undulating scream of a great bird or the anguish of a mourner . . .

He realised it was his own voice he was hearing. He was crying. And Michael had taken his arm.

'Home, Ben. You're still exhausted. There's a kind of shock to these things. You need rest, and then you can come back. I *promise*.'

'Did you arrange to meet her, Ben?' Annie asked suddenly. 'Is that why she was out there?'

'Not now, Annie,' said Michael. 'We'll sort it out . . .'

'Sorry,' said Annie. She sat down abruptly and looked at them helplessly. 'It's just . . . I should have . . .'

'We all should have.' The voice came from someone by the window. 'She was sleepwalking. *You* warned me she was wandering in her sleep, Annie. You know that's it!' The figure moved closer, and through the blurring in his eyes, Ben saw she looked like Annie, only younger.

Something clicked in his mind.

Margaret! *Margaret!*

But Margaret had come already . . .

'This is Kate,' Michael explained, 'Iona's aunt.'

Kate smiled at him.

His brain fought to take it in, to sort the twisting chaos and

105

to calm the drumming in his head. *Kate. Not Margaret — not the girl who jumped and yelled to greet him on the pier. Kate.* Iona's aunt, Annie's sister, who'd stayed at the house to be with her, but hadn't known what he knew . . .

I didn't tell them. If they'd known, they could have stopped her.

He pleaded, 'I woke up and knew Iona was going there, I don't know why, I—'

'Explanations later,' Michael stopped him. 'Annie, Kate, we'll get going now, and then I'll be back here all the faster.'

Explanations. How could he give explanations? He pulled away from Michael's guiding hand. He stood by the bed and looked at Iona. And watching her still, closed face, it seemed that across the glens and mountains and the colour of the intervening days, he could hear the slow, shifting swell of the waters in the bay as they had been that first morning. He could see the dark bulk of the boat. He could see the wheeling flight of the bird and hear its mewing cry thread the mists . . .

And from this distance he could see what he had not seen then – the cords of *Sea Hawk*'s binding hold on her – the shadows that tied her to the ruptured boat.

Then he had wondered what she was looking at, or listening to, or searching for. Now he knew. It had been a kind of waiting. For the spirit of the boat, or the spirit of what was in the boat, or the spirit of what moved restlessly in the deep waters of the loch, that roamed with the seals and rode with the porpoises before the storm.

In its agony it was in *Sea Hawk*, and in Iona – and it was calling to him too.

He knew these things. And yet for all that, he knew nothing, and his ignorance defeated him.

It had the power to grip the loch, wrapping ordinary lives in an unfathomable gloom. He thought of the obscure unease of the Old Village, its darkness; he thought of the old man Calum that Ferry-Bob had talked to there, and Calum's friend, the woman Jeannie – these two who'd never left the place and would probably never leave. And he thought of Kelda's watchful curiosity about the boat.

Here, miles from its place, it held Iona. It overwhelmed the hum of traffic in the streets, the crisp smell of disinfectant and polish in the hospital, the all-seeing lights, the precision of machines and medicine and knowledgeable nurses and doctors. It swamped them all – none of this could erase its hold on her. None of this could bring her back.

He could not tell if it was of the past or of the future. He had thought his dreams were memories, yet now these memories were happening again. He knew things, yet he did not know them. He could not fix the broken pictures of his brain in any shape. He wanted to will her to open her eyes, will her to come back to them. Yet he did not know where to begin, where to find the pattern in what was happening and draw her out of it.

Helplessly he looked at Michael. Michael's eyes met his. And then quickly they switched away.

In misery Ben thought, *Michael's not listening, not hearing, not seeing* . . . and the loss of Michael merged with the loss of Iona and threatened to paralyse him.

Numbly he watched his uncle move away, pick up his jacket, prepare to leave.

Then Michael paused. For a moment he stood there. He turned back sharply and looked at Iona. Something unreadable passed across his face. It was like a spasm. Whitened by the ward lights, his face seemed furrowed and drawn. He put up a hand and pushed hair off his forehead. And it was suddenly a gesture of preparation. He seemed suddenly to notice the jacket in his hands. He put it down again.

He looked at Ben.

For the first time since Ben had stepped off the ferry all those days ago, he felt his uncle hold his gaze. Michael did not switch his eyes away, as if distracted, as if hurrying to evade. He gazed simply, steadily, at Ben. And Ben gazed back, and he felt then as if a kind of bargain flowed between them. It seemed to say to him, we're going to find a way out of this, Ben. We'll find a way to put this right. Somehow. Between us. You and me.

Then Michael came across to him and put an arm around his shoulders. He turned Ben around, and propelled him away towards the door.

This time Ben accepted it. For a brief moment he looked back at Iona, Annie, Kate. He thought of the small smile Iona had given him as she climbed into Michael's van. He seized the memory of it and held on fiercely. And it was that smile that he held on to through all the days that followed.

Sixteen

The journey lulled him. He was cocooned by the jolting rhythm of Michael's ramshackle van. Windscreen wipers swished, the radio murmured, houses and shops, then trees and hills drifted hazily by.

Traffic on the roads out of town had been heavy and slow. At first he'd felt the pull of Iona in the hospital and wanted to turn back. Once clear though, they'd sped along the main road to the turn-off to the lochs, started the climb on the single-track road into misted hilltops. For a time then, the air and space released him from the relentless weight of Iona at the back of his mind.

Not even the sheep moved in the driving rain. They huddled at the roadside, nudged reluctantly from the tarmac's warmth by the van easing past. Michael drove with silent concentration. From time to time he glanced at Ben, as if checking. And Ben half dozed, half gazed at the passing landscape. Try as he might to think clearly, he could only wander in and out of possibilities – a bewildering meander that took him round and round and left him nowhere.

At some time he woke from a deeper sleep and his cheeks were wet as though from crying. But he could not tell why – a dream, or Iona, or the renewed dismay that began to seep through him as the road dipped and the glen floor widened towards the elbow of the loch and the ferry crossing.

It brought new thoughts of *Sea Hawk*. In his mind's eye he saw the boat alone on the bay. Waiting for them, for their return, for their help.

Help for who? For what? How could they ever work this out? In the hospital he'd seen a look of resolution on Michael's face. Had it really been there? Or was he just conjuring what he wanted to see – fabricating a sense of hope?

Michael's closed-faced absorption with the driving told him nothing.

Would Ferry-Bob be at the ferry? Did Ferry-Bob *know* what had happened in the night? With surprise Ben registered that it was only yesterday Ferry-Bob had come to the cottage and told him Michael and Annie were delayed. A century seemed to have passed since then.

Only two other vehicles queued for the ferry. No one got out. Rain spattered noisily on the van roof. The loch was grey and flat, hill colours dull. Cars squelched off the ferry ramp – mainly working traffic. Incessant rain was keeping holiday-makers away.

'At least the ferry's running again,' commented Michael. 'Heavy seas stopped it yesterday.'

There was no sign of Ferry-Bob. It provoked a new

gloom, and Ben realised Michael was looking for him too, winding down his window to enquire as they were signalled into place on the deck. The ferryman moved quickly between the cars, selling tickets, punching buttons on the ticket machine below the dripping folds of a cape that tried to shield him from the rain. He nodded a greeting at Michael and took the proffered money. 'Ferry-Bob's not working today, Michael.' He sorted change from his money belt and bent down to peer through the van window at Ben. At closer quarters Ben recognised the lean, lined face inside the hood: Andy – he often worked the ferry shifts with Ferry-Bob and had come to the cottage once with him.

Smiling now, Andy said, 'Glad to see the lad's all right – we've been worrying . . .' He straightened, handed change and ticket to Michael, 'Ferry-Bob's off with Kenny's wife Helen – to sort out things for Annie – what they need at the hospital, you see. You'll find him at the big house, no doubt.'

'I'll go up there,' said Michael. 'Tell him if you see him, Andy, won't you, I'll be going back up to the hospital in the morning. I'll take anything they want. I promised Annie.'

With a tilt of his head, Andy acknowledged this. He went forward to raise the ferry ramp. The loudspeaker crackled: '. . . *safety notices are displayed on this vessel. Please take note . . .*' Engines rumbled, the ferry churned back from the shore. And Ben thought of the first time he'd crossed here. He'd been on foot. He'd got off the bus, walked down the road, strolled on to the waiting vessel. He'd felt something new, different, special awaited him. It was even in the air he breathed.

Now . . .

Suddenly the van felt dank and dark. He was cramped by the journey. He needed to get out, stretch, feel the wind. But the rain pelted down and in midstream the winds gusted sideways so that the van began to rock. He had a fleeting sense of another deck, another storm – for a second it was with him, then gone again, and he was left with only rising panic at knowledge he ought to have, things he ought to *see*. He turned to his uncle. 'I—'

It lapsed into muddle, unfinished. Curiously, Michael scrutinised his face. After a moment his uncle offered, 'Let's stop at the ferry pub. Get something to eat, sort a bit of this out? Jamie does a good solid line in sausages and chips and in this weather he'll have a fire going. What d'you say?'

Ben nodded. It was a relief. The prospect of the cottage was clouded with the events of yesterday. He was grateful not to have to face it yet. He was grateful the pub was brightly lit and crowded: midday lunches, people sheltering from the weather, a warm fug misting up the window-glass.

Children rambled noisily about the family room at one end. Jamie was kneeling, stoking the fire as they came in, his round face red with warmth and effort.

Michael pointed Ben to a seat by the window and followed Jamie back towards the bar to order food.

'It'll be a minute or two,' he confirmed, sitting down with the drinks. He regarded Ben with a long, straight look. 'I don't want to nag, Ben, but make an effort to eat properly. It'll help to keep your spirits up. We need our spirits up . . .'

Despite the nurse's efforts, Ben had eaten almost nothing in the hospital.

He was worrying more about the clutter in his head. Another puzzle, another blur was confusing him, and he asked now, 'How did we get to the hospital?' Strafing lights and voices he remembered. Nothing else.

He watched Michael take a long drink and look at him over the glass. 'You don't know?'

'No.'

Michael absorbed this. He said slowly, 'Well, you were in bad shape . . . Thank Kenny for hearing you shouting. He found you struggling up the cliff path. You made some sense – he could work out that Iona was also down there. He was already out looking for her, you see. Kate had been having a late bath and then she went to check – panicked when Iona's bed turned out to be empty, scared, because Iona's been wandering about at night. Did you know?'

It wasn't really a question. Michael had halted and stared off into space as if something new was occurring to him.

'Michael . . .' Ben began.

'Kate woke Kenny,' Michael continued as if he hadn't heard. 'They got help up from the village. People were searching – all over. The Rescue did the rest: helicopter lift to the nearest hospital. We got back to the house after they'd taken you off, turned the car straight round and drove up . . .' He pulled a face. 'Had to go the long way round – no ferry. The whole day, night – whatever – one way and another, bit of a nightmare . . .'

113

'Yes,' said Ben. Meaning yes to knowing about Iona's sleepwalks, yes to the nightmare.

The outer door opened. It let in a gust of damp wind and Andy shaking rain off his cape. He yelled his order to Jamie. He spotted Michael and Ben and called, 'Did y'hear about the other boat, Michael? Came up on last night's storm – bit like your old wreck. There it was, aground on the headland for us all to see this morning. Big old fishing skiff it is – they're pulling it off later.'

Startled, the memory obscure, unfinished, but strengthening as soon as the words were out, Ben blurted, 'I saw it.'

Michael raised his eyebrows in a question.

'It came up underneath me. I had to row out of the way.'

Michael considered this and frowned. 'Are you talking about last night? You were out on the loch?'

That stopped Ben short. *He doesn't even know that.* I've not explained even that to anyone.

Where was the rowboat? Had no one found it? And Iona's canoe – *Ulaidh*?

Michael wasn't waiting for any answer from Ben. Instead, across the chatter from nearby tables, he called, 'D'you have an idea where they'll bring this wreck in, Andy?'

'I heard . . .' Jamie's head poked from the kitchen. 'I heard tell it'd be the long shore at the Old Village.'

'They reckon it got pushed in from the main loch, though,' Andy volunteered.

'No!' For some reason it was important to make his uncle

hear this, believe it. 'It was somewhere out in the middle, by the Old Village.' Ben combed his memory of the night on the loch. In that rain and dark, *had* he seen it?

'Do you want to go along there?' Again Michael's question forced attention. Ben tried to focus on Michael's insistent, 'Has it got something to do with all this? Do you think it has?'

Did he? Did he? Why? Something nagged, like a word he couldn't find, like those irritating conversations with his mother when she couldn't remember the name of a film but wanted to tell him all about it. And suddenly it came, like a curtain swept back to show a theatre scene. That first day – the terrible day: scouring the loch for Iona; the calm – that mesmerising silence smoothing the water, the porpoise coiling round him.

The wreck – the fishing skiff. It was stirring then. I felt its beginning. That *was* its beginning.

Ending! he wanted to shout. *Ending – it is the ending, not the beginning – wrong, wrong* . . .

His head was bursting. The chaos inside it. He had to fix the place.

Remember.

The Old Village, distant across the end of the loch, the line of the cliff behind, the ruined lighthouse on the bluff towards the loch mouth, *Rudha Dhubh* too far away to see . . . he drew a picture in his mind.

He said quickly to Michael, 'I do know where the skiff was. I know where it came up from. I saw it rise. I really did—'

'OK, Ben. OK. Stay calm. Do you think it's important? Is it connected?'

Again the question stopped him.

Was it?

'Maybe . . . I think so.'

'OK. OK – that's good enough for me. So we'll go along and look. Yes?' With a new air of decision, Michael picked up his glass. 'Eat, and then we'll go.'

That was where it began. There in the loch. In the middle of the loch. Did I start it? Did Iona? He wished Michael would stop looking at him with that worried frown.

Two plates of sausages and chips were lowered to the table. Jamie leaned across and clattered knives and forks on to the table. He said, 'Forgot to say, about the phone-call, Michael, last night, late. Didn't leave a message, just a name and number. I wrote it down.' He dug a folded paper from his shirt pocket, checked it, handed it to Michael. Then he slid a large envelope from under his arm. 'And this. When are you going to get a phone, Michael? And when are you going to stop pretending you're not living where you are. *Then* maybe people can send letters to your house, not mine. *I* wonder if I'm harbouring a fugitive.' He winked and grinned at Ben. He dropped the envelope on the table. He wandered off to collect up plates and glasses.

Ben stared at Michael. His uncle's face was ashen. He didn't unfold the paper. He just put it on the table, with the envelope.

116

It sat there between them, filling up the space with questions.

Ben asked, 'Aren't you going to look?'

'I don't need to. I know who phoned.'

His expression was stony. *It's not really going to change*, Ben thought. *Now he'll talk to me about Iona, but he still won't talk about this.*

In a rush, because he wanted to admit it, it felt wrong, he told Michael unhappily, 'I saw all the letters in the drawer. You never open any of them.'

'I know what they're about.'

'But someone wrote them. *They* want you to read them.' Now he felt reckless – it wasn't anything to do with him, yet it was. It was like a sort of squaring up. You and me, he wanted to say. You were thinking it in the hospital. Now I'm thinking it. You're *making* me think it.

Michael regarded him. There was a pale blankness to his face. Then he shrugged and looked away.

It was an illusion, thought Ben. It's just like it was. Miserably he picked up his fork and stabbed a chip.

Unexpectedly Michael leaned past him, reaching for the envelope. In a swift, sharp movement he slit it open. He slid out the contents – another envelope. He put it on the table.

Ben looked across at his uncle. Then in a rush he decided, and picked up the envelope. The address was the Canadian one – he recognised it from his own letters to Michael last year. He said, 'Someone's forwarded it from Canada.'

Michael regarded him steadily for a moment. He took the

envelope back and tore it open. There was a photograph and a postcard inside. He looked at them both. He handed them both to Ben.

'Read,' he said. With a flicker of apprehension, Ben wondered if he was angry.

In a large, untidy scrawl, the card said, *'Michael – Great memories. Great times. I'm coming back next summer. Hope to see you and the others then. Thought you'd like this memento of sunny days. Joe.'*

Michael had picked up his knife and fork. He put them down again. His hands were shaking.

Ben looked at the photograph.

It showed three dinghies racing towards the camera. The photo had been taken from another boat, its prow jutting up in the foreground. There were two people in each dinghy. He couldn't really see the faces, but he thought they were probably the same as in the other photo, the one he'd found in the drawer.

'Joe wouldn't know,' came Michael's voice. 'If he did he wouldn't write that. Joe's in the third dinghy there. He left the camp early. The two kids in the first dinghy – the girl and the boy. Thirteen years old. Dead, Ben. Thirteen years old and both dead. They drowned, Ben. While I was looking after them.'

Seventeen

'You think you'll get away from it. I thought here'd be good – start up fresh, blank slate, new horizons. Leave it behind. But the more things roll on, Ben, the more you see them coming back to look at you. Like a circle. I thought that when I saw Iona lying in the hospital. All you do is put it off for a while. In the end it tracks you down . . . and sits there till you stop and look at it.

'How to describe it? Brilliant day. Sunny, brisk wind, nothing difficult. The lake looked beautiful. I wasn't on duty. My boss, David, was. But he wasn't around. He never was around. Thing about David was he wasn't ever where he was supposed to be. Never read what he was supposed to read, never answered messages left for him. The rest of us covered for him – we'd been covering since I got there a couple of years ago. Every time, every thing, the rest of us covered.

'We had these kids on a three-week residential sailing course. Good kids. Enthusiastic. Fast learners. They'd all made the grade – got various qualifications, various levels, some of them pretty advanced dinghy sailing stuff. Come the last day, most of them packed up and were going home. Some of them wanted to go out one last time.

'We had this rule – *no one out on the water without specific permission*. There was always supposed to be full lifeguard lookout, rescue boat at the ready. That day the kids couldn't find David to ask. So they just took the dinghies. I saw them going. I didn't see David, but I didn't check, just assumed, had half an eye on them – the way you do. But only half an eye. Even that went because Rachel turned up.

'Rachel had been a friend for a while. But she'd been away for a week and I'd missed her. I was amazed how much I'd missed her. Hadn't expected it. We were going on holiday together the next week. I was beginning to suspect we'd end up married by the end of it. Beginning to think it was what I wanted to do. And a whole lot of other things – about her, the holiday, what I was going to do afterwards. I wasn't watching the kids or the water. I wasn't thinking about David, who was still invisible, and *that* probably meant he was somewhere else and maybe no one but me was looking out for those kids. Didn't stop to think maybe they'd been silly, the way kids can be – over-confident with their new skills. Thinking they'd be all right – you don't need a lookout and rescue boats and the like – not for a quick sprint round the lake and back. They were all high on having their qualifications. Full of knowing what they were doing. Just kids . . . doing foolish things sometimes, because they don't think what might happen next.

'First I knew, Rachel said, "There's a capsize. Something's wrong, the kids are waving."

'One boat was down. The other two were up, and seemed to be trying to come in close to the capsized one. We got out there, that's when I woke up to it being just us, no David around, no one else. The kids were crying, yelling. They'd tried to right the dinghy, it went right over again. They'd done the drills on the course, *knew* what they were supposed to do. But they were just kids . . . not ready for this kind of mess. Two kids missing. Barbara'd just disappeared, Tom came up after the capsize, and then went down again to look for her. He didn't come up again.

'Rachel went in – she's a strong swimmer, trained diver. She found Barbara straight away. Trapped below the sail, caught up in the rigging. Sort of strangled. And drowned.

'We couldn't find Tom. Didn't. Not till late evening, already dark. His body'd drifted off in the cross-currents.

'The inquest said he'd taken a blow to his head. Somehow in the panicking and the kids manoeuvring to get the boat up, he probably got hit.

'I didn't get sacked, Ben. Technically I wasn't on duty. David was sacked; there was a long enquiry. Afterwards I was offered his job, because there were records about my efforts to complain about the place, the way it was run. The way *he* ran it. People kept telling me it wasn't my fault. I wasn't supposed to be there. I could have been anywhere and then I wouldn't have known it was happening and wouldn't feel guilty.

'It's not that easy is it?

121

'I *knew* David was idle, lazy, a coaster. Rode on other people's efforts. I argued with him about things. It got me nowhere, slid off him like I never said it. I was worried about the boats being in rotten condition. We needed funds to repair them. The bungs were perished. Buoyancy tanks had no covers. Lifejackets were faulty. The point is, when it came down to it, those kids shouldn't have been on the lake in those boats at all. And the point is, I argued for a while, even wrote letters to head office about more funding. But in the end I gave up. I did some repairs myself, but not enough. I just began to trust to luck and the fact that the rescue boat was around. Put my head in the sand.

'When those kids capsized they *should* have been able to get the boat righted easily. But they had difficulty because the open buoyancy tanks filled up with water. And then when they did start to get the dinghy up, the water slopped about and pushed it over again.

'I tried to tell myself it was just a dreadful accident. I started by going along with the verdict – David responsible for the disaster, the poor state of the boats, the whole bit . . . After all, I'd been saying something needed doing, hadn't I?

'But when they offered me the job, something just went. It was an accident waiting to happen and I *knew* it was waiting to happen. I just pushed it aside. That afternoon I was so busy talking to Rachel I pushed it further away than usual.

'In the end you have to turn and look at it – see it for what it is. I let those kids down, betrayed them. Betrayal. That's what it is. There isn't another word for it.

'The letters are from Rachel. And the phone calls. Rachel won't accept I've left and don't want to go back. She wants to pick up where we were. But it feels like she's all mixed up in what happened. I can't get round that. It's gone all wrong, sour, scary . . .

'I came here, thought I'd start fresh, get a new job. I started to apply, but never finished . . .

'I can't go out on the water any more, Ben. I did try. But all I see is that dinghy submerging, and the look of Barbara when Rachel brought her out from under the sail. I see Tom's body when they brought him in that night.

'Thirteen years old, that's all they were. Joe doesn't know anything about that. He left the day before. There was another kid who left early, who sent photos. I got them a few weeks back. She didn't know either. Someone at the office there's being helpful sending on the letters for me. Probably someone new, probably doesn't know about any of it, just come up for a nice summer job. That depresses me too. I wonder if it's just returned to being the mess it was, and there'll be someone like me there who'll fiddle at trying to do something, then wash their hands of it because it's too difficult, needs too much energy, because it's *easier*.

'So what now, Ben? What to do? What to do – you and me?'

So many signs along the way, Ben thought. He'd seen only the fussing. He'd been irritated by it – he remembered being irritated. He remembered Michael watching as he roamed with Iona in *Ulaidh*. He'd resented it a little: the questioning, the inspection of canoe, lifejackets, capsize drill. Scrutiny to the point of frustration – why did his uncle not believe; he didn't seem to trust him on *anything* – he remembered thinking that.

But he'd felt low about resenting it. As if not liking Michael at those times was disloyalty.

'I've got things to do,' Michael always said when they asked him to come out on the loch with them. 'You go ahead: that's fine.'

Ben went cold, remembering. Michael was just too taken up with *Sea Hawk*, he'd thought. In a way, he'd sulked a little.

His uncle had always stood on the shore as they pulled away. He'd put the binoculars to his eyes. He always had binoculars. To look at seals and birds, Ben assumed.

Now he saw those random memories welded together by Michael's story. Not a fussing Michael, but a scared Michael. Afraid when they were out. Nervous when he couldn't see their boat. Trying to keep track of everything, yet not stop them, not cripple them with his private terrors.

Ben said quickly, because now it was important to say it, part of the partnership, part of the deal between them, 'I keep having these dreams about someone drowning. About someone *drowned*. I thought it was going to be Iona last night.'

He told him then. He began at the end, and then moved back to the beginning. And as he talked a little more came from the shadows and took shape in the light.

Eighteen

They'd left the pub. They'd driven along the loch and stopped above the bay. Michael switched the engine off. *Sea Hawk* lay below, dark in the rain-gloom, trussed in canvas against the weather.

Ben held back. 'Michael . . .'

'Just going to check the covering, Ben. You don't have to come – stay put in the dry.'

Ben shook his head. Now he was sick with foreboding. Some part of him had drawn Iona out towards the deepness of the waters – he'd felt it, *known* it then. Part of him was calling now, a trembling echo born as they entered the long, flat curve of bay.

Yet it was a call stirring far beyond his hearing, a long way off. It was distant, drawing nearer – towards its beginning or its ending, he could not tell which and the dread of it swamped him – dread for Iona, for himself, for Michael now. The anger had nothing to do with him, yet it throbbed in his veins, grew through every part of him . . .

With a sudden stark clarity that blasted through confusions

he said, 'It's someone else, Michael — not always, not everything, that's where it's muddled, but often, more and more and more, it's someone else . . .' and the jumbled debris of his dreams swirled out — tangled words and pictures — hopes, terrors, loves, he was in them and watching them and fearing them, 'Real things, Michael, they happened, I thought they were memories, then I decided they weren't because of what happened to Iona, but now I know they are, they belong to someone else, trying to make it happen all over again — I don't know what—'

'Slow down.' Michael had half-opened the van door. Now he slammed it shut again. 'Slow down, Ben. I *am* listening — I know I haven't been, and I'm not a great one for believing this kind of stuff. I like my explanations clear and simple — something I can get hold of. But I don't need convincing there's something here that needs a different kind of looking at—'

The closing door shut out the rain. It seemed to Ben that it shut out the echoes too. Inside the van was very quiet and calm and strangely warm. For a while Michael said nothing. Then, as if groping towards something, 'Know what went through my mind in the hospital? I thought — Ben's been worried about something. I knew it, you even told me. I think I knew you were really depressed, maybe about Iona, maybe about something else. But it was easier to write it off — moods, quarrels. Easier not to look too hard . . . like not looking too hard at all the other stuff either — Canada — all that. Haven't felt like looking at anything too hard . . . But back there in the hospital, I thought, Iona's nearly drowned, she's badly hurt, and if I'd stopped, focused – just a bit – I might have spotted this was brewing. Been able to stop it. Maybe.' He fell silent.

Ben began, 'But I should—'

His uncle put a hand on his arm to stop him. 'Annie's thinking that too, I guess. She was worried, but she didn't really hear Iona. She's always in a panic about losing the job . . . lets that boss of hers keep her on the hop with it. He thrives on keeping everyone on the hop . . . Likes playing at being lord of the manor—'

He rubbed the misted window and stared out at the bay. They watched a bird glide in to *Sea Hawk* and alight on the bulge of the canvas. Wings stretched, folded, and the figure was still. Beyond, on the distant ridge of the boulders, the huddled lines of the cormorants.

'I suppose . . .' came Michael's voice again, 'people died in *Sea Hawk*, Ben. I don't *know* that they did, but it's a reasonable guess. It's all very well restoring it, making it look good. But maybe we shouldn't forget that people died. Maybe we have to find out about that. Maybe that's what it's all about. Maybe we'll have to tell the boat's story. Maybe *Sea Hawk*'s story and the other boat – this wreck of the big fishing skiff that's come up in the storm – are somehow tied up together. Ben, what d'you say? Maybe that's where we'll find the starting point?'

The rain had slowed to a drizzle. On the shore below the Old

Village people had gathered, a knot of spectators under hoods and umbrellas and lower down the beach men checking the winch carefully and laying ropes and wires for hauling.

Ferry-Bob was helping heave the rollers into place, ranging them in a line to receive the wreck. Beyond the breaking surf it floated, roped steady to several anchors.

Boots crunched up and down the shingles, scattering pebbles. The air rang loud with shouts.

Ben slowed, and hesitated. Again the foreboding trickled through him, a dismal, nervous urgency.

Michael threw a questioning look at him. But Ben couldn't answer, and so Michael halted at his side. Together they stood at the top of the beach and watched.

A loud hail from someone at the winch, answering calls from others on the beach, a general bracing on ropes in all directions and abruptly the skiff moved forward, water pouring from the bows, long curves sweeping from the water to meet the rollers, gliding on to them, mounting the steep bank of the beach with the steady pull of the winch.

Much bigger than *Sea Hawk*. Colours lost. Not a modern boat, glass fibre and smoothly moulded, but wood planks, solid, big, built for heavy seas and long hauls to the fishing grounds. Ben had seen photos of fleets of skiffs like this with their crews of three or four or even five. In one of Michael's books. He remembered scanning some of them the day he'd waited at the cottage. Only yesterday.

The skiff was out. The men braced it with wooden legs and chocks. Everyone stood back in groups. A few peered into it and under it and ran hands along its sides. Now there was a reluctance to talk or move away, except for the yapping puppy that belonged to the visitors and the children running with him.

Ben began to walk towards the skiff.

Michael, he realised, as if from some great distance, had left his side and gone to talk to Ferry-Bob. He saw them turn and look towards him. He saw them begin to walk in his direction.

He went on down the beach, towards the skiff.

There is a stillness in it. It wraps him, and with it comes the deep cold shroud of the sea.

He stands below the prow. It rises above his head, dark with moisture, rich with the smell of the loch. He does not touch, yet he feels it on his face and the palms of his hands, and the skin of his arms and his legs, on the soles of his feet. He feels its coldness now and its warmth on other days, and the tilt and roll of it beneath him.

'*Sea Moon*,' he whispers.

'Ah,' says someone standing near him. 'Ah.'

It is a word of assent. Ben sees it is the old man, Calum.

'Aye, *Sea Moon*,' Calum says to Ben. 'That it is.'

'What are you on about, Ben?' Ferry-Bob is urging insistently. 'Calum, what's all this? There's no name on the boat, Ben lad. That's what they're talking about, down there. There's nothing left of any name for us to tell it by—'

'It is my uncle's boat. It is mine,' murmurs Ben. 'It is *Sea Moon*.'

PART FOUR

LACHLAN

Nineteen

'It *is* the ending,' he told Michael, later.

Beginning, ending – how could he know? How could he know the skiff was named *Sea Moon*? After, he would wrestle with the questions, just as Ferry-Bob and Michael pressed and urged and watched him worriedly. He found no answers.

Perhaps he knew it from the old man Calum, beside him at the skiff, hunched inside a coat that dwarfed him, fingers picking restlessly at buttons. He'd glanced at Ben and then away. He'd muttered something and begun to wander off. He'd moved unsteadily, distracted. He'd returned to look again, shaken his head, muttered more . . .

Maybe it was Kelda's fall that told him. He had not seen her on the road above the beach until a quickening consciousness made him look up. Too far to see her face. Agitation stiffened every line and angle of her body. A woman argued angrily with her, a short, round, dumpy woman dwarfed by Kelda's height. Kelda was shrugging off the woman's words, eyes only for the skiff, pulling from the woman's restraining hand, hunting for a route across the steep-banked boulders and down on to the shingles.

Mesmerised, Ben saw her abruptly stumble forwards, lurch, heard the woman's startled shout, saw Kelda crumple, fall, lie still – no longer tall and proud and straight, but frail and crooked across the stones.

One man had picked her up, hoisting her weight as if she were a child. The woman led the way, hurrying to her nearby house, across the road. Behind came the anxious convoy: Michael, Ferry-Bob, others Ben didn't know. They stood about while Michael found the phone and called the doctor and the woman showed where Kelda could be put to bed. She found a cover, stayed to try and stop the frantic murmuring, the fretful movements. Blood trickled on Kelda's arm, bruises darkened her face already, she moaned as if in pain. She mumbled endless names that no one knew: Archie, Angus, John. She wasn't making any sense.

Someone else came hurrying after them, chased everyone from the room, took charge. Helen, someone called her, and Ben realised that this was Kenny's wife.

'Broken something, I don't doubt,' said one man. 'Too old to break her limbs, our Kelda is. They don't mend the way they should – not when you've said goodbye to eighty-four.'

'Eighty-five,' said someone else. 'Strong woman, though, she'll be going for years yet, she will.'

Silence fell. They crowded in around the two worn chairs and television and the little table, filling up the room with unspoken worried expectation. Helen came from the bedroom, gave orders for the doctor to be rung again. 'She's hurting bad. He's got to get here quick, tell him.'

Michael went into the hall to do it.

'Helen'll do fine by her,' said someone approvingly. 'She was a nurse before she had her kiddies. It comes out in her bossiness.'

Outside the rain had stopped. A fragile brightening was spreading across the loch.

In here, the light has never reached, thought Ben, not to this room. It wasn't the smallness of the window – he felt the shadows like a touch across his skin.

'All these years.'

The murmur came from Calum, standing at the door. Puzzled, they all turned and looked at him.

He wandered to the window. He stood unsteadily and rocked a little as he looked towards the skiff. 'They said it was gone and he with it, but they were wrong, it wasna' gone. It wasna'. *I* knew. I did.'

'What are you on about, Calum?' Ferry-Bob asked. 'Come and sit down, man, and stop talking in riddles.'

'The skiffs out for the scrubbing, and the ballast spread to clean, and *Sea Moon* dead on the beach, dead since it happened, and none of us going near . . .'

'If you're going to gabble, Calum Finn, you can gabble in your own house,' said the dumpy woman sharply. She stared at him from her chair. Belligerent defiance set a scowl on her face, and he returned the look, set-jawed, eyes wide behind his glasses.

135

'Aye, but it's there, Jeannie, it's there and *you* know it is.'

She made a clicking sound with her tongue and jumped up angrily.

'Jeannie, Jeannie,' Ferry-Bob said to her. 'Calm, not so quarrelsome now.'

'He's going to gabble, he is. Blether, blether.' The woman's voice rose shrill with argument. 'He's not to go on like that, I tell you. He'll go the way of Kelda . . .'

'I was twelve,' Calum told them with certainty, ignoring her. 'I remember clear . . . I was a lad of twelve. We had to stay away – all of us that were left, and then in the morning it wasna' there, and people said good riddance, it was all for the better now it had gone and he with it. I remember clear I do . . . after. I *remember*. All the skiffs, they stayed there, weeks and weeks, no heart for anything, no heart to do the work . . . And then *Sea Moon* wasna' there any more, and they said good riddance to it.'

Ferry-Bob stood up, planted himself squarely in front of the old man. 'What are you saying, Calum? You know the old boat down there?'

'I do. Archie MacKay's skiff, that is.'

'See!' Jeannie shouted. 'Twelve he says! He doesna' remember *anything*. Ten, he was. You're gabbling, Calum Finn, and she's gabbling and you're going to bring it on us all with your nonsense!'

'You're doing a fair bit of gabbling yourself, Jeannie, when it comes to it . . .' said Ferry-Bob. 'But she's right on one thing,' he told Calum, 'you're still not making any sense.'

'That he's not,' someone else agreed.

Jeannie sat down with a bump, and looked around. She insisted, to no one in particular, her voice rising with emphasis. 'I was *nine* and he was *ten*. He should remember that because we couldna' go. Alexander could because he was *eleven*, it was his birthday that very day, and we were very cross he was to go without us. You *remember*, Calum, we were so cross and they promised that we'd get our chances the next week, all together. If—'

The woman, Ben saw, was crying. Calum was crying too.

I know them all, Ben thought. I remember a sunny day of celebration. Bright colours. Calum, Jeannie, Kelda, Margaret – others – on the pier. I know them now and I knew them then – nine and ten years old, and all the years before and all the years between . . .

He said quickly, no time to hesitate, 'There was a pier . . .'

'No pier now,' said Michael. 'There used to be. I've seen a picture, somewhere . . . A bit further up the shore, I think.'

'Long gone,' someone added from the corner of the room. 'Before my time.'

'Fine wooden pier it was,' Jeannie murmured. Tears glistened on her face but she hadn't wiped them. 'New. We built it, all of us. He had us working at it all through spring and summer – him up at the big house there. We had to get it ready for the steamer.'

Michael looked across at Ben.

'I can't make head nor tail of any of this,' someone

complained, but quietly. 'And who's Archie MacKay anyway?'

Calum sniffed and nodded through the window towards the shore. 'It's his skiff there, it is. Archie's. He fished it with two others. And his nephew too – the young lad that—'

'Y'r brain is addled, Calum Finn!' Jeannie broke in fiercely. 'You cannot know that's Archie's skiff—!'

'Did a bit of piloting too, when there was a call for it, did Archie,' Calum went on stolidly. 'Been dead awhile, though, Archie had, when *Sea Moon* went away. The pilot, Archie was, on the night – it was him that took the steamer on the rocks.'

Ben felt very cold.

'*He* should know about Archie,' Calum added forcefully, nodding at Michael. 'And him, there, too – the lad. It's Archie's cottage by the headland you're in, man. Always seemed to me a fitting place for a man who took a steamer on the headland rocks.'

Twenty

The light snapped on.

'Ben, *wake up*.'

He was being shaken violently. He struggled to leave the sounds that drowned him.

'*Ben*. Wake up! You're dreaming!'

Frenzied shrieking. Terror, he could hear the shrieking terror above thunder, screaming gales . . .

'Up, Ben. Out of bed. Pull on something warm, it's gone very cold. Into the sitting room. Come *on*, wake up. Let's do this right – I'll make something hot to drink. *Don't* go back to sleep. *Ben*.'

'Michael—' He lurched awake. The panic clung to him. 'OK, OK. I heard—'

He hauled himself upright. His head refused to clear. He fought the muddle, drugged with noises.

He tried to focus on hunting for his tracksuit. He'd dumped it on the floor beside—

What had he seen? The rocks, just as before. The rocks at Shallachain House.

But something else was there, just out of reach. He sifted pictures – it lurked too dimly at the edges of his vision . . .

He found his clothes and pulled them on. He stood up to go into the sitting room.

A boat.

He sat down sharply, dizzy with the sudden movement, dizzy with the image, dizzy with the effort of remembering.

Sea Moon? No. Too small.

Not the steamer either – too small to be a steamer.

Not on the rocks – he saw that suddenly. Tossed in the waves, swamped – steep-breaking seas reared up behind, crashed down across it. Thunder, lightning flaring, then all dark again . . . Dark, very dark.

Look back, look back. A final, savage swell . . .

He sat very still. He did not dare to move.

Finally, he'd seen it.

Finally.

In the time between, hearing his uncle moving in the kitchen, he recognised several other things, sorting them in his head to make something clear that he could tell to Michael.

'It's *Sea Hawk*. Our boat. *Sea Hawk*, Michael. I know it is, Michael. It's not the wrecked fishing skiff *Sea Moon*, or anything like that. Or a steamer. It's *Sea Hawk*, but it's not anywhere near the headland where you found it. It's right up the other end, on the rocks below Shallachain House.'

Michael stopped in his tracks across the sitting room.

'OK.' He put two mugs of tea on the table. He went back to the kitchen and came out with a pad of paper and a pencil. He sat down at the table.

'Right – straight, now. Fact on fact. I don't want frills. Think reporter. News. Tell it straight, just like it is. Ben? You see why we have to do it?'

He focused on his uncle's urgent tone. He concentrated, wanting to match Michael's determination, dredging from the scraps that whirled about his brain, the threads he'd suddenly been able to grab and knot together. With all his mind and body he wanted to be able to stand back from them and see the pattern. He began, speaking very fast, '*Sea Hawk*. Me. My uncle – it's not you, Michael. I can't really see him but I *know* he is my uncle. *My uncle*.

'Eight, nine other people. More, maybe. Girls some of them, women, men. We're rowing the boat straight at the rocks, trying to get close. We're swamped, boat's plunging and bucking, standing vertical in the waves, going over. My uncle's yell – *jump*, he yells. I jump, and I'm on a rock, clinging, sliding down. I look back – the boat's gone. Nothing – just black water.'

He finished, breathing hard. He hadn't said what it felt like. Couldn't say what it felt like.

Michael sat looking at him. He had written nothing.

He said, after a while, 'Do you really know the rocks? This is dark – at night? It's a storm, you said.'

'Yes, but then it's dawn coming up. It's not the same dream, but it follows. I'm still on the rocks. Wet, bleeding,

141

trying to scramble up. That's when I see the girl. She's rolling in the surf . . . it's the girl I keep seeing, and this time I know her face, she's from the boat, I saw her before. I try to lift her up, try to pull her out, but—'

Michael put the pencil down. The page in front of him had stayed blank. He said slowly, 'Maybe you – whoever – were unconscious between the two times?'

Ben sipped the tea and thought about that and shrugged helplessly. The chill was getting to him. Even the glow of lights couldn't give any sense of warmth to the room. The smell of the water lingered in his nostrils.

He got up and went into his room and found a pullover.

In his absence, Michael had begun to write. A page of single words with circles round them, arrows here and there, scoring out and underlining. 'You know what I've been thinking, Ben. I'm not sure – but think about this: Iona moved here in the New Year. Early spring, she started wandering about the loch. Then *Sea Hawk* appeared out of the blue – sticking up in the sand. Maybe there's something there. Could there be? Maybe it began with Iona disturbing something?'

More, Ben thought. It's *more, much more*. But why did he feel that? It was beyond him, and he didn't say it to Michael. Instead he said, 'I didn't know this wasn't her place. She never mentioned.'

'They lived down Oban way before. Since her father was killed, anyway. Before that they lived somewhere else – I'm not sure where the family comes from originally.'

Ben said nothing. He was thinking that there were a lot of things Iona had never told him.

He said, after a while, watching Michael writing, 'I didn't know her father was dead. I assumed he'd gone off and left them – something like that.'

Michael looked up. 'No. He was killed five years ago, give or take, though Annie talks like it was yesterday. He was a deep sea diver on the oil rigs. There was some kind of accident – several divers killed. Annie's never got used to it. Maybe she won't ever – she's scared about being alone, about not coping. Iona doesn't talk about it, but I get the feeling she was very close to her father. That's who taught her to sail, you know. When she was very young. I think that's why she's so keen on the water.'

'Which boat are you on about now?' demanded Ferry-Bob. 'It's bad enough keeping up with old Calum and Jeannie, without the two of you making riddles too.' Since he'd arrived he was in an unfamiliar mood, irritable, his thatch of hair unusually dishevelled, dark-eyed with fatigue.

'*Sea Hawk*,' explained Michael. 'This is all *Sea Hawk*. Our boat – the one *we* dragged out of the sand, you and me. Keep your mind on that, Ferry-Bob. Listen – in the spring Iona got the canoes out and cleaned them up. I gave her a hand – you remember – *you* suggested it. If you think back, Ferry-Bob, we found *Sea Hawk* not long after Iona began canoeing up and down. Don't you *think* there's something there? Doesn't it make a funny kind of sense?'

'I wish something would make a bit of sense,' said Ferry-Bob wearily. He ran his hands across his face and stretched. He'd arrived early and stomped into the cottage loudly, thinking he would be waking them. Feeling the need to get on and sort things out, he said. 'I've been up half the night at Jeannie's place . . .'

'She's no better, then,' said Michael, meaning Kelda.

'The old girl's rambling. The doctor didn't want her moved to her own place yet. She's very bruised and battered, hurting a lot. Not just the body, either. Long stories no one can make head nor tail of. All about this old skiff up there – your *Sea Moon*, Ben, and about her brother Angus, and he's been dead awhile and moved away years before that, there was no love lost between them by all accounts, so why now—'

'It's not just about *Sea Moon* and *Sea Hawk*, it's about the steamer too, Ferry-Bob,' Ben interrupted him. That much was clear to him. He'd got up early and walked along the shore to try and shed the clustering shadows. He wanted to find the images again, separate them from the nightmare wakings, the plunges in and out of dreams, the sombre fears. It was important now, he knew, to try and pick them clean and place them in the open for all to see.

Kelda was a part of it. And now there were others too – Calum, Jeannie, Archie MacKay, others he might not know about – the ones that Kelda talked about, for all he knew – the Anguses and Johns.

He insisted to Ferry-Bob, 'You see, I've dreamed about a

steamer.' He repeated, numbering for them all, 'There's *Sea Hawk*, and a steamer, and the skiff called *Sea Moon*. They're all three mixed up in this – somehow.'

Ferry-Bob looked despairingly from Michael to Ben and back again. He shrugged. 'We-ell, mebbe you're right and mebbe you're not. I can't see how you knew that old skiff's name, that I can't, and you're saying the daftest things. We're not going to get much sense from that lot in the Old Village, I can see.'

He sat down, and for a while he was quiet, thinking. 'You know, I've not thought of it for years, but all this brings it back. I remember my grandfather telling about a steamer as went down in these parts. I don't remember properly. It always seemed a dark kind of story to me. He never finished the telling – always wandered off in the middle. He wasn't from round here, so I can't be certain.'

'Wouldn't there be newspaper records?' said Michael. 'We should have thought of that.'

'The newsletter!' Ben leapt up. The pile of magazines and books was on the table, just as he'd left it. Quickly he searched and found the newsletter, opened the page and read the sub-title: *Hamish McLean tells of bygone days*. There was a blurry picture of several skiffs beached on a long, flat shore. All a bit like *Sea Moon*. He showed the piece to Michael. 'Whoever wrote that might know something . . .'

'Now *there's* a clever thought,' said Ferry-Bob, his voice lightening. 'Let's have a look . . . There y'are,' he announced triumphantly. 'You're a genius, lad. That's our man all right.

Hamish has more scraps of history stuffed in his head than he knows what to do with. *He'll* know, if anyone does.'

'There's a contact address,' Michael showed him.

'No good. That's an old issue, see – last year. Hamish moves about a fair bit. But there's sure to be someone can find him. I'll do that, that I can do.' He was vastly cheered by the prospect of something practical to do. Now he hesitated. 'Are you going up to Annie at the hospital, Michael?'

'I'll go too,' said Ben.

Michael began to protest and changed his mind. '*We'll* go,' he confirmed.

'I ask,' explained Ferry-Bob, 'because there's something else needs doing here. There's a call to sort this business of the old skiff out. It's not just Calum and Jeannie and Kelda all upset. There's several others talking. The old ones, you see, though there's only a handful left. Michael tells me you saw the skiff come up, Ben. There's a call to get some divers out and see what's there. The police want to know if you'd be willing to show where you think you saw it, Ben. I said I'd ask. They'll put a marker down, and mebbe come back later to have a look.'

Ben didn't answer. He only knew that he didn't want to do it, didn't want to have to go out on the loch again. Not now, maybe not ever.

'It *is* something we could do,' said Michael. 'What if I come out there with you? Ben? We'll do this one together?'

146

Twenty-One

He opened a window and leaned out. Wet tyres hissed in the street below and sunlight was breaking through the cloud. He sniffed the unfamiliar warmth, thought of the colours of the days he'd spent with her.

She lay very still behind him. He'd tried to sit there. He'd watched, waited, willed, begged. But for all the scraps of information they'd begun to put together, there was still no reason for what was happening to her, or why. 'No change,' the nurse had told him. 'But that's also good. Your friend's not getting any worse, and that gives the doctors time to find out more.'

She'd smiled – trying to reassure him. But every click of the clock hand in this long waiting time was another threat, unnameable . . .

He remembered Michael saying, 'You have to name it sometimes. People are always superstitious about naming fears, possibilities – in case they *make* them happen. But sometimes it's the only way to make them go away. Or to deal with them.' And he'd laughed. But it was a laugh without much humour. 'I'm a great one for giving advice on naming fears, aren't I?'

Name it.

Too many deaths were lingering at the edges of this story. He didn't want to name another one.

Yet since he'd returned and stayed here with Iona, Ben had recognised a peculiar calm. The racing memories had quietened. As if by shaping some of them, giving them logic, life, they'd brought a lull, a pause in the headlong rush towards . . .

Towards what?

There was one puzzle he couldn't put aside: he knew who'd died on *Sea Hawk* – he'd *seen* them. But whoever's life he was sharing, remembering – that person hadn't died that day. He held Iona now. It was what the person wanted. It wasn't all the person wanted, but it was part of it.

She might not die, but she might not ever wake again.

The fear was something solid, like a wall that blocked him from moving forward.

Climb over it. He could imagine Michael saying that.

How? How?

He turned and looked at Iona's face. It was closed to him, to all of them. He thought about the smile she'd left with him. He thought about her bottomless fund of information about the loch, the tides, the winds, the birds and seals. He'd thought she was extraordinary, always knowing everything. Now he saw her missing father in it, her private homage to him, her way of filling up the absence she never spoke about.

And was Michael right? Had Iona's endless passing to and fro across the face of the loch begun to stir *Sea Hawk* to life again? And *Sea Moon* too?

Or was it me brought *Sea Moon* up?

He had wondered if all this began that day he'd knelt and looked into *Sea Hawk*'s ruptured side and felt the breath of the boat flow over him. But maybe there were several beginnings – for Iona, for himself, for Michael even, though Michael had not seen it, too full of other memories he struggled to obscure – Canada, the kids' drowning on that distant lake.

Ben dropped into the chair beside the window. He wished Michael would get back. It had been difficult to persuade Annie and Kate to go away, to shower, change, walk in the air – break from the hours of vigil they felt compelled to keep. It had taken Michael to prise them away with promises he'd see them to the hotel he'd booked. He'd also try (he said it quietly to Ben) to track down newspaper archives. 'Worth a try, I think. Just a first quick look. I'm not going to say anything to Annie, not just yet. Let's get it clearer first, or it becomes something more for her to be scared of.'

Now Michael had been gone a couple of hours. When would he be back? Fears were different when you could talk about them, less of a mess to flounder in. More nameable.

He came to thoughts of the watching seals later – the porpoise, the cormorants waiting for the tides, the birds that wheeled about the bay. Had the creatures of the loch been guarding Iona, trying to guide her? Did they sense the hidden pattern that impelled her forward? Or were they a part of its power, driven by its energy, strengthening its will with theirs?

He didn't like to think of them like that. She wouldn't either. She would argue fiercely in their defence. He smiled at the thought. Once she'd been furious with him for saying the buzzards looked so savage, dropping with such deadly aim down on some hidden, unsuspecting prey.

'Savage!' she'd snorted. 'That's a *people* word! People are savage. They *choose* it. Animals just do what they have to . . .'

A light footstep sounded behind him. Annie had entered the room. She looked scrubbed; fresh clothes. But her face was just as pale and just as tired.

'Michael's on his way, Ben. He's just talking to Kate.'

'You didn't need to come back yet,' Ben said. 'I can stay with her. And Michael.'

'I know, but it's my . . .' She didn't finish, and he could hear resignation – more, defeat – in her tone. He wished he could tell her *it's going to be all right*, like they did in films, and you knew it would be because it *was* a film.

She stepped aside to let two nurses in. They brushed past her and in a flurry of movement whisked the curtains closed round Iona. 'Sorry, people, we have to push you out now. Things to do. Won't be long.'

Seeing the sudden anxiety on their faces, the other explained less brusquely, 'Just for a while. We'll give her a wash, and generally see to her . . .'

150

'I can stay and help,' said Annie.

'No, no. We have to turn her and massage her legs and back – it'll all help to keep her right and comfortable,' said the first, more gently.

'I want to stay,' insisted Annie.

'No.' More firmly. 'You go off with your friends. Have a cup of coffee downstairs? Back in half an hour, we'll be done by then.' She said it meaningfully to Michael and Kate, arriving at that moment.

Michael was swift to take the hint. Briskly he ushered them to the lift and down to the café in the hospital entrance hall. It was an airy, high-ceilinged room, landscapes of lochs and mountains on yellow walls, long windows letting in a watery sun, loud chatter.

They took their coffee to a table by a window, settled down, and then there was a pause, and Michael exchanged a look with Ben.

Looking for something to talk about, thought Ben. Something to ward off the dispiriting, vacant mood. The spectacle of Iona, washed and turned and pummelled like some lifeless doll just sat between them all and refused to go away.

Mustering his own determination, Ben looked at Annie and asked, 'When was the fire at the house?'

'Yes,' agreed Michael. 'Tell us a bit about it, Annie.'

'Why?'

'Just asking. Curious. I only know some of the story. Snippets.'

151

'Well, I don't know much. It burned down. No one ever found out why. Or who.'

'Any idea when?'

She shook her head.

'You *do*, you know,' her sister corrected her. 'I remember you telling me, Annie. Some time in the thirties . . . 1933? A summer night, you said. *He* told you, that fellow you work for.'

'I don't remember all the details,' repeated Annie.

'Well I do, like I said. She told me,' Kate assured them.

'Why are you asking?' Annie wanted to know again.

'No reason. Really. I've meant to ask before. I'm just interested generally, Annie,' Michael insisted. 'Don't find worries where there aren't any . . .'

Ben wondered if Michael felt as bad as he did, pretending. He'd told him about the dreams of fire and the house.

Kate was saying, 'There was some story. Your boss liked it, Annie – you remember. You told me he fancied himself as this fellow all over again.' She'd latched on to the conversation – a way of filling up the space with something other than Iona. 'The fellow who owned the place then, the laird or some such, he was giving a party. Apparently he liked to give big parties. Had a bit of a reputation for doing something special, glamorous, all the time. Had people travelling a long way to them. But this time, he got much more than he bargained for – the house burned down during the night. No one died or anything like that, but the biggest mystery of all was the laird fellow just went off. Disappeared!

152

They never found any bodies in the fire, and then after a while they knew he wasn't dead, because he sent word he was going away and wouldn't be back. Off he went, and that was that. Never an explanation. You said it was the anniversary of some disaster . . . You remember, Annie! Surely! You said there'd been some talk of the disaster and the fire being connected. At the time, I mean. Rumours and gossip and the like. Nothing came of it. At any rate,' she concluded, 'the place was uninhabitable after that. It went to rack and ruin pretty fast. It's been a ruin as long as *I* can remember. Always seemed very sad, I thought.'

The dream of fire bothered Ben particularly. It was a thread he couldn't connect with other images – the wrecking of *Sea Hawk* on the rocks, the dead girl in the water. Yet it was this dream Iona shared with him.

Now, listening to Kate, watching her face, it brought sudden thoughts of the other fire he'd dreamed about, the flames – not the flames of Shallachain House but the flames of the cupboard, not a cupboard, but the door of a furnace and a man stoking it, the flames leaping white-hot, the burn and roar filling the air, and he turning to greet Margaret . . .

Margaret. A new thought entered his head. *Annie, Kate.* He'd thought he knew Annie, that first time at Shallachain House. And he'd mistaken Kate for Margaret, when he first met her beside Iona's hospital bed.

They all look alike.

Quickly, before the chink of understanding closed, before

he could change his mind, he asked them both, 'Do you know anyone named Margaret?'

Annie shook her head.

'You're being daft, Annie!' Kate said to her. 'Our granny's name was Margaret.'

Ben sat back. The meaning. There it was. So simple, somehow. Was this it? Annie's grandmother. Iona's great grandmother. Was this really it?

Michael was looking at him curiously. Ben hadn't told him about Margaret. It seemed too complicated, too muddled up. Now he wished he had.

Kate said to Ben, 'She's been dead for years – twenty at least, or even more. Why d'you ask?'

'I came across the name the other day,' Ben said hurriedly. 'I think Iona mentioned it.' The blood rushed to his face – he'd never been much good at lying.

'Iona wouldn't have known her,' said Kate. '*We* didn't see her very much. I remember my mother saying she was difficult. She went very odd when our grandfather died. She didn't live long after he went, I don't think.'

'It's been half an hour,' Annie fretted. 'I should go back . . .'

Michael sighed. 'Not necessary, Annie. Give yourself a break.'

She didn't answer. Just getting up, and giving him a half-smile. 'I don't mean to be rude, Michael. You've been kind. I'm very grateful for the help. But I want to be there. Just in case—'

Kate exchanged an unhappy look with Michael and followed her sister out.

In the long, depressing silence that followed, Michael and Ben stared down into their empty coffee cups. Then Michael straightened up and said decisively. 'I didn't make much headway at the library – with the newspapers, I mean. I looked through stuff, but I wish we could pin down the date. I didn't think to ask exactly how old Calum and Jeannie are. In their eighties I imagine – so if they were nine and ten when the steamer foundered, if you work it back, that would make it the early thirties. I started looking in 1930 – that seemed sensible. But nothing found. Haven't given up, though.'

'1933?' said Ben. 'Kate said the house burned down in 1933.'

'But she said it was an anniversary of a disaster. Maybe the disaster was the steamer and the house burned down a year later.'

'The steamer was the year before, then,' Ben suggested.

'1932? Worth a try,' Michael brightened.

After a minute, he asked carefully, 'Why *did* you ask about this Margaret, Ben? Is she important, do you think? You didn't say anything about her before.'

'She's someone else I've seen on the pier. But it's not that, it's more the feelings – like you said with you and Rachel in Canada,' Ben finished awkwardly.

Michael scrutinised his face. 'Ben, *don't* select what to tell me and keep back other bits of it, or we'll never get to the bottom of this. We *have* to get to the bottom of it. If what's happened to Iona is tangled up with all these things you've seen, it may be the only way . . . *I* don't know and *you* don't know what's important and what isn't.'

'Just – sometimes it's so confused.'

Michael nodded. But Ben could see that he was waiting.

'The Margaret *I* see seems to be a friend of Kelda's,' he said. 'I can't work out anything else. She looks a bit like Annie. Very like Kate. Sometimes she's muddled up with Iona—'

There was another silence while they both thought about that.

'Well,' said Michael finally, 'it does make a kind of sense then, if there's a resemblance. Doesn't it? Iona's great grandmother?'

'But you said they weren't from round here. And wouldn't Kelda *know* they were related to her friend? She's never—' Ben began.

'I forgot to say about Kelda,' Michael interrupted. 'I rang Ferry-Bob to ask how she's getting on. First, though, he's got hold of a phone number for Hamish – the one who writes those pieces in the newsletter. Hasn't spoken to him yet, but will. And Kelda – well, apparently she's not too good. Still hasn't said what she was trying to do – rushing to the skiff like that. Not making sense. But she's asked to see us, Ben. You and me. To tell the truth, I've been expecting it.'

Twenty-Two

'I said I'd track him down and here he is.' Ferry-Bob produced his companion with an air of pride. 'Hamish!'

Hamish McLean grinned broadly. He was a burly man, tall, bearded, not what Ben expected. Though what he did expect he couldn't have said.

Hamish shifted a plastic carrier bag from one hand to the other and shook hands with both of them. He held the bag up for them to see. 'I brought you what I could. I had to hunt about a bit, found it in a box up in my sister's place. I'm sure there's more – somewhere. But I dug out what I could in a hurry. Ferry-Bob said it was very urgent, so here I am.' He glanced around the room. 'Didn't Ian live here, a while back?'

'Still does, on and off,' said Michael. 'Just loaned it to me while he's away. We've been friends for years – since college.'

'Well . . .' the other man answered, and Ben wondered if he stored even that away for future use. He watched him tip the contents of the carrier bag on to the table. Two brown

157

envelopes, a battered notepad, a few small scraps of paper. Then Hamish sat back and looked at them, as if considering where to start.

'I gather there's been a wrecked fishing skiff come up from the bottom of the loch.'

'Don't know if it's connected. Possibly is,' Michael told him.

'Well, you tell me when you do know.' He picked up an envelope and pulled out a sheet of paper. Numbers were scrawled large and bold on it in thick red ink. Ben leaned and looked. *1932*. Behind the paper, secured by paperclips, were yellowed newspaper cuttings.

But once started, Hamish was quick and to the point, delivering his information without a look at cuttings or notes or anything else he'd brought.

'My father knew about this steamer,' he said. '*I* came across the story when I was looking into something else – a long time ago. I asked my father what he knew. He wouldn't say. Wasn't from round here, you see, but he'd heard talk of it. I remember him disapproving of my questions. He said too many died to make a story of it, it didn't bear the looking at, as far as he could see, wasn't to be meddled with. So I never did. I'd gathered scraps, but when he took on like that, I put them away. I've wondered now and then, but I've never looked at it again – not till Ferry-Bob asked.'

'But you can tell us what you know,' said Michael anxiously.

'Not much. Some of it just hearsay, too, so you'd need to

check. I've got one or two cuttings from the newspapers of the time. I can leave them with you. From what I gathered, the Old Village up the loch here was going through a transformation. That was the plan, anyway. Some fellow came back from abroad with money and schemes to put the place on the map – help it to "greet the modern world", was a phrase he was reported using. It's in one of the cuttings, if you look. Bring in regular steamer runs – cargo runs for carrying stuff to the bigger markets, and some special runs for the visitors. He had plans to start regular, fancy steamer cruises in time. Get this loch on the excursion route . . .

'They called this fellow the laird – but he wasn't. William Dunnell: third son of a fourth son – so really the grandson of a laird. He got the estate up here as a grant from his grandfather. Dunnell had been off to university, wasted a fair bit of money, failed his exams, got packed off to Africa – Kenya, I think – to see if he'd make good. He must have struck it lucky there – he came back with money to spare and ideas for starting something big. Make his name as a reforming landlord, I fancy was his dream. If the truth be known, calling him "the laird" was a sort of joke on him, and maybe he knew it. Ideas above his station, if you see what I mean. He moved into the house up top, and made it very grand. Had all sorts of bits and pieces shipped up here specially. (To tell the truth, he reminds me of the fellow that's up there now, fancying the place up. Though there's no connection – I checked on that.)

'This Dunnell started work on the village and the villagers.

That's in the newspapers. He put some money in and raised the rest by "public subscription". What *that* meant was a few wealthy friends, and the villagers with their savings, any that had them, that is. The rest just put in their labour, and lots of that.

'Anyway, the plan was to put up a pier: one that could be used by bigger boats, and at all tides. And to put a light in the loch. Nothing fancy, you understand, just a simple fixed light – enough to guide the steamers through the channel past the headland. You can see the ruins of it across the loch there. The light was very important, because without that he would never persuade anything big to risk coming in. The reefs and ridges under the headland were notorious. And there's the islets that cover over with the tides . . . I don't need to tell any of you about all that, living here as you do . . .

'Dunnell must have had a way with him. He persuaded a steamer company to add this place to their regular run. Maybe they were happy to, because he put in money enough to give one of the smaller paddle-steamers a face-lift and a new name. One *he* thought was more appropriate.

'On the first run of the steamer from this pier, there was a freak storm. The steamer went down on the rocks. Or maybe it foundered on the islets. Thing is, no one knows. Scraps of it drifted in on the tides. And the bodies. No one survived.

'I did find a photo of it leaving that day.'

In the silence, Hamish opened the other envelope. '*Maid of the Glens* was the new name, used for the first time that day, and never again. But I remember finding out that it was an old steamer that had been doing a regular run for years on the lower lochs.'

He put the photograph on the table for them all to see.

'There it is. With its new name, of course. Its earlier name, I found, was *Sea Hawk*.'

There he stands, beside the paddle-box. Bright-faced, hair blowing, tall above the others crowded on the deck. He is with an older man, and Ben knows that it is Archie – his uncle, Archie. Together, they are looking up, and Archie points towards a lifeboat suspended high above the deck.

'*Sea Hawk!*' Ben hears Michael say. 'But that's the name of *our* boat. It's not a steamer!'

Ferry-Bob says to them quietly, deliberately. 'I should have seen it. They always name lifeboats after the main boat they come from. Always. Then, if they're separated, it's known which vessel it belongs to. I should have seen . . .' he says again.

Michael murmurs, in disbelief, 'Our *Sea Hawk* is the steamer's *lifeboat*?'

There he stands. And his name is ringing in Ben's head – and the name is in the voice of Archie whipped off by the wind, yet calling to him still across the years.

Lachlan.

161

Twenty-Three

'She's been wanting to see you since the morning,' Helen told them. 'She's been terrible since we got her back to her own place – restless, never sleeping. Not the Kelda I know, I can tell you. Always been a quiet woman, keeps herself to herself. But I can't leave her alone now, Michael. She's trying to jump up all the time, shouts out for you. Won't rest till you're here – says it's got to be done if it's the last thing that she manages, whatever *it* is. I've been trying to get her to sleep, but it's beyond my powers. She won't go into bed, not till you've been.'

They'd stopped outside the room. Helen pushed the door wide open and switched on the light. Kelda dozed in a chair, wrapped up in rugs, propped about with pillows. But she was shivering, and at the sound of their arrival, her head snapped up.

'Michael, Michael, to my shame, I never told! To his shame he never told—'

'Kelda,' said Helen gently. 'Let them get in first, and sit themselves down properly. They'll hear you all the better.'

She switched on other lights. She moved the radiator a little closer.

Yet a chill gripped everything. Ben wanted to hear what Kelda would say, and feared it. He felt as if a trembling disturbance was passing from the old woman into him. He wondered if Michael felt it too. He thought of Calum and Jeannie and the others Ferry-Bob had talked about, all worried by the rise of the old skiff *Sea Moon*. And he wondered if this was the same obscure distress as they were suffering.

They sat down in the chairs that Helen had put ready. Kelda, silent as they did so, almost dozing again, jerked suddenly upright, dislodged rugs. And for a moment there was a flurry of movement while Michael tucked them round again and Helen wedged the pillows firm.

'Where's Ferry-Bob?' Kelda demanded of her.

'You didn't say you wanted him here too.' Exhaustion was thinly masked in Helen's voice. 'He's outside, Kelda, but I thought you said just Michael here, and Ben.'

'No, no, Ferry-Bob too – everyone, everyone . . .'

But then, as if forgetting, not pausing while Helen fetched in Ferry-Bob, Kelda began to speak. Low-voiced, so quiet that they had to lean forward to hear what she was saying.

'Eighteen I was,' Ben heard her whisper. 'Just turned eighteen. Margaret – she was seventeen . . .'

Afterwards, it was the monotone that Ben remembered, the suddenly calm, expressionless voice. As though she recited something long learned by heart, long, long rehearsed. She's told it to herself a million times, he thought, in preparation for the day she would tell someone else. And then she never had.

Afterwards it was the images that stayed in his mind, the pictures flickering, filling his eyes and ears with colour, texture, sound, all fed by Kelda's murmur: all drawn from some deep reservoir of memory that was not his, belonged to someone else, yet filled him now as if all happened yesterday.

Sunlight glistened on the paddles' wake. Bright dresses like a beacon shining from the pier – Margaret. Kelda. He remembered thinking, standing on the steamer's deck, waving to them, seeing Margaret's laughing merriment, *she should be here with me.* He remembered her joyfulness, showing her round the engine room. This is what I'm going to do, he'd told her. I'm going with the steamers, and you'll come too. She'd laughed at that, and not believed him . . .

'It was a very happy time,' Kelda told them. 'So many possibilities, new things, hopes, plans. We were all to be married soon. Me before the summer passed. Me and John. And in the autumn, Margaret was going to marry Lachlan. We were so full of plans – so full of hopes. So much was going to happen when the steamer came.

'The steamer would be changing everything. Imagine it. Our little loch – just the fishing and the crofting, and not much else. Days and days it took to get to anywhere else, except by boat. But now we had a steamer coming. Every week, and sometimes twice, and (who knows, they said) maybe more times than that, there was no knowing what might happen.

'His idea it was, him up at the house. William Robert Dunnell. Full of big ideas. Pier, lighthouse, steamer. All through the spring and summer it was all any of us had thought about.

'That first day was to be a special run. A big opening. A celebration. At midday the steamer would arrive and bring William Dunnell's friends in for his celebration party. Then the rest of us – all of us from the village – were to go on it. And in the evening it would bring us back. The morning after, it would leave again, carrying William's friends away. Until the next run, the week after, and the week after that . . .

'Not everyone was going on that celebration run. Not the children. The children were to go with our mothers later. But most others went aboard, everyone who'd helped build the pier, everyone old enough to go alone. My younger brother went. My John's sisters too. All the girls and men from the cottages in the village and beyond. People gathered from up and down the glen, oh, everyone wanted to go! Just a very few men had work to do and didn't join it. My John didn't. Nor my brother Angus. Nor their friend Donald. I didn't know why it was they didn't go, what it was they had to do that day. I didn't know it, then—'

'Mainly this was our special day, us younger ones. We dressed up in our party finery, and off everyone went, to board the steamer. A new beginning – that's what people felt it was.

'I didn't go, or Margaret, but only because we were in service at the house, and William Robert Dunnell had his party to get ready for. Oh, the excitement! The excitement of the steamer and the excitement of everything happening at the house. We'd not been working there for long, you see, either of us. We'd been taken on a few months back.

'We thought it was very glamorous. Margaret especially. There were all the guests to look at in their fancy clothes. Fancy food, fancy furniture. We had time enough to see the steamer off, just to rush down and wave from the pier, and then back up to the house . . .

'I remember Lachlan standing there. High up on the deck. So pleased he was! Lachlan was fascinated by that steamer. Already he'd made friends with the steamer captain, he was that full of questions. That morning, before they let the passengers on, he was given leave to show Margaret the engine room and furnaces. Margaret came back full of it. He'd told her how he wanted to go on the steamers – look for work on them. Later, when she told me, we joked about his uncle, Archie, that he'd never let him go, the two of them had always fished *Sea Moon* together. Archie'd be a hard man to persuade and what Archie thought mattered something terrible to Lachlan. He had no other family – lost years back, and he'd only ever been with Archie that he could remember.

'The steamer sailed. The weather was so clear, so bright. Lachlan's uncle Archie was on the run to do the piloting. He knew the waters like his own hand, he did, though after, they tried to say he didn't. But Archie knew every rock and channel and sandbank of our loch like he knew the boards of his own boat. He was a fisherman you see . . . tides and winds were the things he marked his life by.

'I remember how they steamed away. Music playing and flags fluttering, and the dresses brilliant in the sunshine, and us cheering, and Margaret jumping up and down on the pier so Lachlan could still see her, and we watched them out of sight and then we turned and raced as fast as we could to the house, chattering all the way about it.

'We never knew what happened. In the morning, there was only Lachlan on the rocks below Shallachain House, confused, babbling about the lifeboats going down and everyone with them, about seeing Archie go, about following the light . . .

'And that was a terrible mystery, how he could have been following the light. Because, after, when they looked at everything and tried to understand it, they found the light had failed. The light had never worked that night – not ever.

'Five or six bodies came in on the tides. They drifted in to different places on the loch. Most of the ones who steamed away that day, we never saw again.'

'People died on the steamer. But on the shore we died too. It's never left us. It's never left the little ones whose brothers and sisters went down that day. It never left our mothers and fathers. They carried it with them till they died. For some it became a twisted thing: people began to think it was the excitement had brought it on. The steamer and the lighthouse and the glamour William Robert Dunnell was going to bring. It seemed like the steamer going down was punishment for all of it.

'And with Lachlan being the only one to come out of it alive, and him so fascinated with the steamer, and his dead uncle, Archie, being the pilot on that night, people began to look on Lachlan to blame. He'd lived when others died. His uncle Archie made the mistake. Him up the house, William Robert Dunnell – he was the hardest of them all.

'I didn't know the truth of it all then. But I remember thinking that William Dunnell's harshness was a very odd thing.

'Margaret – well, Margaret – I think she loved Lachlan. But when the mark was laid against him, she was different.

'Months later, after Lachlan had gone away, she told me that he'd come to see her on the night he left. He asked her to go with him. He wanted her to help him find a new place. To start again. Fresh, you see, without the stain that people put on him. He wanted to take *Sea Moon* and go, and take their chances in the world together.

'I remember what she said to him. I'll never forget what Margaret said to him. She told me afterwards. She said she shouldn't be seen talking to him. She said she didn't want to make William Dunnell angry. She said that William Dunnell thought Lachlan wasn't a fit person to be talking to, seeing as how his uncle was the one to put the steamer on the rocks.'

Twenty-Four

The room was very quiet. Kelda's eyes stared from the pallor of her face. Yet the voice was steady, growing steadier.

'I didn't know the truth, not at the beginning. There was an enquiry, but no conclusion drawn, not an official one. Just a dreadful set of accidents that came together, they said: just a storm come up from nowhere; the new light failing.

'For William Dunnell there was no doubt in any of it. He said the fault was to trust to Archie to do the pilot's work. It was Archie made the mistake and lost us everything.'

Now Kelda stopped. They shifted in their chairs and thought that she was finished. Helen got up and offered her a drink. She waved the glass away. 'No!' she insisted sharply. 'I'm not done!'

But it was minutes before she began again, and they waited silently, and Ben's thoughts went back to Iona in the hospital.

A new, wavering fear was mounting in him. He had begun to understand the anger.

'Margaret saw a future in working at the house,' Kelda said.

'Oh, she was fascinated by the comings and goings there – people from distant places. There was talk of William Dunnell marrying and she had hopes of travelling with his family. She filled her head with notions.

'That night the steamer went, I lost my taste for William Robert Dunnell's house. I couldn't abide the thought that while we'd been dithering about with food and music and dancing in a grand house lit up like a Christmas tree, all that time, down on the water, in the dark, there'd been that terrible thing happening. I lost my taste for lots of things that night.

'And I didn't know several things I wish that I had known. I didn't know that Margaret saw Lachlan the night he left. She didn't tell me till many months had passed. I just knew that Lachlan went away and no one ever saw or heard of him again. He took *Sea Moon*, and off he went. But now, you see, there's *Sea Moon* in the loch . . .

'Margaret married someone else. She was my friend, but after she told me about that very last time she spoke to Lachlan, we never talked very much again. And then we never talked at all. She left here when she married. I never knew where it was that Margaret went to . . .'

There'd been another long silence, stretching for minutes. Kelda had closed her eyes. Helen got up and leaned across to look at her. Michael and Ferry-Bob stood up and thought about going.

Ben stayed sitting – Kelda's stillness was not a peacefulness,

170

it was a preparation – he knew it, he felt the agitation growing . . .

'John,' she said without warning, harsh and loud. And words came tumbling in a torrent, rushed and breathless, 'After the steamer wreck my John became very strange. We were all strange, but he was worse than anyone. He seemed to die that day, just stopped everything, stopped talking to me, stopped seeing me, even when he looked—' She paused and breathed very hard, and suddenly thrust her hand out to a sheet of paper on the table at her side.

She held the paper, crumpling it with the tightness of her hold, and began again. 'A few months after the wrecking, John also went away and never came back. He's somewhere still for all I know, or dead. His family never heard from him again. I never married him, and when I didn't I could never bring myself to marry anyone. I closed a door and I never opened it again.

'He lost his sisters on the steamer. I lost my younger brother. My elder brother, Angus, he changed too. He'd been good friends with John. And there was Donald too. The three of them – Angus, John and Donald – always went together. And together, that day, they'd not gone on the steamer, because of work they had to do, they said. But they stopped being friends after that day. They'd planned to buy a boat together but had never had the money. Not long after, they did buy it, and I never knew where they had got the money, after all. And then John left. Angus and Donald quarrelled bitterly. And then Donald went and married Margaret . . .

'I never understood. Not till years later. And when I did understand, to my shame . . . to my shame . . . I never told . . .'

She'd paused again. She'd fallen silent. Ferry-Bob and Michael stirred, uncertain whether to stay or go. Ben sat still, and waited.

She looked at him. She began suddenly, her voice stronger, as if shot through with new determination. 'John came to see me just before he left. He said I must know why he was having to go away. But what he told me made no sense to me.

'He said he'd gone to Shallachain House to talk to William Dunnell. About something private. He said he'd had harsh words with Dunnell. He said Dunnell threatened him for coming and turned him out. And John had been so angry afterwards that he'd gone back to speak to him again. He'd looked in through the windows and there was Dunnell sitting grandly in his house, holding forth all lordly to his guests, and John had imagined the way he would be telling of his plans and all he would be doing for the village and the glen.

'John told me that the sight of it sent him into such a rage he'd rushed into the side-wing of the house, not knowing what he meant to do. But there William Dunnell came to him and tried to throw him out again, himself, not calling servants to help for fear what John might say to them. There'd been a fight, and John had got the better of him, and in his anger seized a log from the flames burning in the grate and thrown it furiously across the room . . . and then the fire took hold, and he *rejoiced* in it.

'He didn't tell me what the quarrel was about. He seemed to want to. But he kept saying that I must ask my brother Angus. "Ask your brother Angus" – over and over and over. "It's not my place to say."

'I did ask Angus. I begged Angus. He would never say. Never a word.

'We never had a great deal to say to each other, and over the years we had less and less. He moved to Inverness. He died years back, and the lawyers sent his papers on to me. Among them was a letter that he'd never sent. He wrote it to me in 1937. The letter's here. Read it now, Michael. Read it, and let's be done with it, once and for all.'

The crumpled paper from her hand. A single sheet, written on both sides:

I have to write this now. I have carried it for long enough, and I cannot carry it further. I do not know what you will do with it.

I will set it down bald, because that is the only way I know. Make what you will of it.

On the night before the steamer went down, William Dunnell asked me to do some work for him. He needed three strong men to help with carrying. We had to have a boat. It was to be a secret because it had to do with a surprise he was fixing for his guests that night at the celebrations for the steamer, and the opening of the pier, and all the rest of it.

When it came to it, he wanted us to take a generator for making electricity from the lighthouse, and load it in the boat, and put it in his house. This was not the main generator of the lighthouse he wanted, but the second one – the one kept for emergencies, in case the first should fail.

He had a secret plan to stun the world by lighting up his house with electricity like a beacon to greet the steamer coming home. A beacon to a new era on our little loch, he said. The way he had with him – you remember it. Just a bit of borrowing he said, and not for long. The generator would go back next day, safe and sound, and we'd be part of something very grand.

We did not think about it. He asked, and we did it – it was just a bit of borrowing.

It was me he asked, and I took John and Donald with me to do it.

We did not know the light would fail that night. It came out in the inquest that among the terrible chances of that night, there was something wrong with the main generator that made it fail. There was a question why both generators failed, but it was never answered.

I tell you now: both generators did not fail. The second generator could not fire the lighthouse. Because it was in William Dunnell's house atop the cliff, lighting up his party.

When everyone went to look at the lighthouse, the generator was back there, where it should have been.

John and Donald and me were the only ones who knew it had ever left. I took it back, with Donald. John would not do it. John wanted to tell what had happened. But William Dunnell asked us not to say. Not ever. It was only a bit of borrowing, he said. Not meaningful, not useful to talk about it, even if it had gone wrong. It would not have stopped the steamer running aground he said. He was sorry for our trouble and in recognition of the help we'd been to him, he would pay for the new fishing skiff we'd always wanted.

We took his money. To our shame, we took it. We said nothing.

I do not know what you will do with this. But I have carried it for long enough, and now I cannot carry it further.

Kelda's mouth was quivering as she tried to take a drink from Helen and failed. Helen took the glass away and put it down again.

Kelda did not look at Ben, or any of them.

It was Ferry-Bob who broke the silence first. 'The emergency generator of a lighthouse. He stole it, for a party!'

They're wrong, thought Ben. They're still all wrong – somewhere, somehow, this is not all of it.

There *was* a light. He saw it in the mists. High up and wavering, and the steamer *Sea Hawk* driving straight for it.

'They were too far over, far too far,' said Michael. 'The way these things work they'd have seen the lighthouse beam only if they were heading right for the channel, well clear of the headland, well clear of *Rudha Dhubh*.'

'Archie can't have seen a light,' Ferry-Bob reminded them. 'There was no beam from the lighthouse that night. It wasn't working.'

'He did see it,' said Ben. 'The light *was* there . . .'

He glanced at Kelda. He could tell it from her eyes. They both saw it now, the ending, the truth of it.

It was hidden in his own journey across the loch to find

Iona. The light high up. He'd seen it through the rain. The confusion of distance, height. No way of judging anything in the muddle of sound and darkness. No point of reference to tell him where it was.

That night a light had shone for the returning steamer. He'd seen it in the dreams, followed it with Archie, blazing through the storm, high up, followed it with the lifeboat to the rocks of Shallachain House.

Not a lighthouse beam.

The lights of a cliff house aglow for a celebration party.

Not the beam of a lighthouse to draw them to the south-west, clear of the headland, clear of the rocks, into the deep, safe channel of the central loch.

The lights of a house at the end of the loch, that drew them north-west, towards the headland, into the teeth of the rocks that took them.

Kelda sighed. 'It's in the waters. It's never washed away, not for all the tides and all the storms since then. It stains the headland. It stains the shores. It stains all of us.'

Twenty-Five

He'd found the place for them. With Michael he'd led the procession of motor-boats across the loch. Michael kept their engine slow. No one talked. In other boats they held binoculars ready, but stayed behind and waited.

He'd known the place at once. Its restless chill, the deep darkness of the place. It shivered through him, and he said to Michael '*Here*,' even before they saw the shadows turning below the water – *Ulaidh* and Kenny's rowboat moving in the slow green currents, back and forth, round and slowly round.

Michael had turned the boat, called out to others. 'I'll take Ben back – but this'll be the place to look.'

He knows, because he feels it in his bones, what they have found, what they are lifting from the sea and bringing home across the loch.

The cold stays with them. They huddle by the fire in Michael's cottage and try to lose it. But it lingers, and Michael tries to move beyond. 'They'll want to look at everything. Obviously they won't easily accept what we'll be saying. In time they'll work out something. There's talk of murder – ballast and chains and other things wrapped round, you see.'

'It wasn't murder,' Ben says quietly.

'I know.'

'He went himself. He sat there in *Sea Moon*, just took *Sea Moon* from the shore, and went out to the middle, and sat and waited . . .'

'I know, Ben. I know.'

Ben shivers. He knows because he's found the meaning in the memories: the rising water like a shroud about him. The despair weighing like the burden of stones he's taken from the beach and loaded on the skiff for ballast, the bungs he's wrenched from the hull and holds in his hands, the touch and smell and tilt of these boards that are all the barrier between his emptied life and the waters where Archie and the others wait.

'There'll be a record to be set to rights,' said Ferry-Bob. 'We *can* do that, that much we can.'

Michael leaned down and stoked the fire, trying to conjure up more heat. 'Lachlan couldn't have seen the house burn down. It was too long after the night he died – a year or more. That's *if* he drowned the night he spoke to Margaret. John did the burning, a year later. Ben . . .?'

Michael's eyes urged him to leave the silence that had wrapped him since they found the bones of Lachlan in the loch.

'It's just – he gets confused,' Ben said. 'He sees Iona and he thinks she's Margaret. That's partly why – I think so, anyway. I think he remembers the last time he saw Margaret at Shallachain House and he muddles it up with other things he's seen – years and years wandering about the loch . . .'

'He saw the burning after he was dead? You think that's it?' Michael pondered it. 'That makes a kind of sense . . .'

'Unfinished business,' murmured Ferry-Bob. 'It's all about unfinished business. Like this William Dunnell going off, who knows where. If you think about it – it's a right mess he made. Him behind it all, and he turns the blame on Archie and Lachlan. But then he's not the only one to blame, is he? John and Angus and Donald – they should know better than to tamper with a light. Men of the sea, they were, they'd need no teaching—'

'But the light was new,' Michael pointed out. 'There'd never been one on this loch before. Why would they think it was so important, not used to steamers and these bigger boats?'

'Even so,' said Ferry-Bob, and shook his head. 'Even so. I reckon they'd have known. They pretended to themselves it'd be all right. And after, they must have seen the lights from the big house were what the steamer followed. They'd have known. Look at this Donald marrying Margaret – some kind of regret, I reckon. She'd lost Lachlan, lost her work when the house burned down – Donald knew John did that, and it was all mixed up with him and Angus and the terrible thing they did, taking that generator.'

'Margaret *sent* Lachlan away,' said Ben. 'She didn't *lose* him. She turned her back—'

'Head full of stuff, like Kelda told us,' Michael said. 'A silly girl. Maybe she didn't mean it. Kelda said Margaret didn't believe Lachlan's scheme about the steamers. Maybe she didn't believe he meant to go away either. And she was nervous of William Dunnell, of being shut out from all that . . .'

'Guilty for being bedazzled by William Dunnell's grandness?' Ferry-Bob said. 'Well, guilt does funny things. And she didn't know that Lachlan killed himself, remember. No one knew that.'

'Kelda did,' said Ben.

'She didn't *know*. She feared.'

'They all knew he was miserable, and all alone,' Ben said. 'His uncle was dead too. There was just him here after that—' he looked around him at the cottage. He didn't want to imagine that. Lachlan had never shown him that.

There was a long silence, broken only by the sputtering of the fire.

'For Donald it was a peculiar kind of atonement, to marry Margaret,' Michael commented after a while. 'I don't know – maybe for Margaret, in time, it seemed another kind of betrayal.'

Ben left the cottage. He climbed up the path to the headland, taking the route that Iona first brought him on the day of his arrival.

The tide was rising. Distant water sparkling, lapping the outer ridges of the rock. Opposite was the jutting arm of *Rudha Dhubh*, its chain of islets, the nearer ones already washed by the inward racing tide. All that time ago, sitting on *Rudha Dhubh*, Iona had drawn her map for him with shells and seaweed. How little he'd seen then, though he'd looked so hard and tried to learn.

It was important, now, to make some kind of peace with it. With Lachlan, with this place. Soon, when the police had done their work and a conclusion had been drawn, Lachlan's bones would be put to rest. And in some way – too late, too little, but at last – so would his memory.

He thought of Kelda – quieter since the telling, but still wandering in her memories. She no longer made much sense to anyone listening. They'd gone to tell her what was found and taken from the loch. They'd sat with her. But she had not seemed to see or hear them, drifting in and out of fragile sleep. And after a while, they'd left.

'She's going,' Helen said to them. 'She'll not make many more days. We have to see that.'

So there was Kelda's peace to make with Lachlan, too.

Now, on the headland, Ben held the fragment of wood with *Sea Hawk*'s name on it. Once it had been given to him – a message of a kind, he felt. Now he wanted to give it back, return it to the water it had come from.

He scrambled down until he reached the lower slabs of rock. He walked until he reached the water glistening on the dark-seamed outer ridge. For a little while he stood in the freshening wind and looked about him. Then, with all his strength he threw the wood high across the water, watched it fly out, arc downward, seem to gather speed, and plunge.

He felt the release of Lachlan then, and all the others who'd been a part of it, of Lachlan's punishment, the hopelessness of everyone who'd lost – stolen lives piled year on year, tying the village to its past.

Staining the waters, Kelda said.

Yet now it seemed to him that Lachlan's peace was showing in the returning brightness of the air, the burnished metal of the loch, the swell of the waters, gentler in a steady wind. Buzzards mewed on the pine slopes behind the cottage. Gulls and oystercatchers swooped again across the bay towards *Sea Hawk*.

Earlier, Michael had said, 'I'll finish restoring *Sea Hawk*. I don't want unfinished business of my own.'

'*We'll* do it, and then we'll take it on the loch,' Ferry-Bob agreed.

There was no knowing what his uncle would do tomorrow, or the day after that. But already Michael was different. Something beckoned ahead of him, not just behind. And Ben had played a part in that, and that was something.

It was the ending, they'd believed, now that Lachlan had been found. Though neither said it to the other. They'd sped along the bigger, busier roads towards the hospital. They'd been so certain of what they'd find – Iona sitting up, the happy smiles of Annie, Kate. The waiting time all over.

'No change,' the doctor greets them. 'I'm very sorry. We're doing all we can. There's still no clear picture of why, we're doing everything—'

She is inert. Just as she's been ever since the night he'd reached her on the rocks. And the doctor's words have a hollow hopelessness.

Twenty-Six

He has watched, waited, willed, hoped. So has Michael, Annie, Kate. He remembers Kate saying once, 'She's a strong-willed girl, Annie. She'll pull through. She's not going to give up on us and we'll not give up on her.'

They hadn't told them what they knew of Lachlan, Margaret and all the rest. Not yet. 'Time enough when she's back,' Ferry-Bob advised. 'It'll be time enough to tell them then – it'll take some understanding . . .'

We have understanding. It's bringing nothing now for Iona.

And it isn't just Lachlan's story, or Margaret's and the others.' It's also mine. Iona's.

Lachlan found Iona through me.

Lachlan had found their friendship, made it his own, peopled it with memories, hopes, loves, fears -- and anger. At all he'd lost, all that was stolen from him, all that was taken by Margaret and all the others . . .

And yet Lachlan's desolation has left Iona. That much Ben feels. That darkness has left the room.

But there are still shadows here.

The dreams he shares with Iona come into his mind. The memories – Lachlan's memories of Margaret – wrapping Iona in all his love and hopes for Margaret.

The one dream – shouting in the darkness and she running away towards the house. Lachlan, Margaret, their last meeting – she telling Lachlan to go away . . .

There is another: the blazing house, flames way up, Iona'd said – a bonfire reaching to the sky.

He searches his own dream of fire and does not see the girl he knows is Margaret. The flames are close. They sear his skin, they scorch – he has come through them, has run from them—

Ben stands with hammering heart.

These are not Lachlan's eyes.

Not Lachlan's eyes I'm seeing through.

Not Lachlan's memories of Margaret. Not Lachlan's confusion of Iona, Margaret, the living and the dead.

These are the eyes of Margaret.

And with the name the knowledge surges in – not Lachlan's *memories* of Margaret. Margaret *herself*. Drawn here by Lachlan's thwarted love for her, drawn here by Iona, Annie, Kate, their bonds with her, their bonds with William Dunnell's house, living in rooms where Margaret once slept, walking lawns where Margaret watched Dunnell's parties from the dark, with all her tarnished hopes and muddled loyalties.

Drawn here by Lachlan's love and Lachlan's rage at her.

It's not Lachlan's ruin, *his* cheated past that holds Iona. It's Margaret's bleak penance, her final search for Lachlan.

A racing certainty is gathering pace in Ben. Once, Michael told him to name his fear.

Name it.

He looks down at Iona.

'*Margaret*,' he whispers.

Michael turns to him with a startled look.

'*Margaret*.'

He draws all his knowledge of Lachlan to him, Lachlan's loneliness, his fear, his love, his anger. Lachlan, who'd reached out for Margaret, drawing her across the loch to come to him.

Yet *he* would not want *this* now. In his misery he'd taken Iona for Margaret. But now, with all his longing, he would not choose this living death for anyone. This vengeance would not be Lachlan's.

He says again, sending his knowledge of Lachlan, his hope for Iona, surging out against the bitter shadows that are Margaret.

'*Margaret*.'

A new despair is clouding Michael's face. He grips Ben's shoulder hard, begins to steer him away.

But Ben resists – there was a sound, so faint he almost missed it.

A breath exhaled, a breath drawn in.

A life released, a life returning.